PRELUDE TO LOVE

PRELUDE TO LOVE

Nina Tinsley

CHIVERS LARGE PRINT
BATH

British Library Cataloguing in Publication Data available

This Large Print edition published by Chivers Press, Bath, 1995.

Published by arrangement with the author's estate.

U.K. Hardcover ISBN 0 7451 3038 0
U.K. Softcover ISBN 0 7451 3046 1

Photoset, printed and bound in Great Britain by
Redwood Books, Trowbridge, Wiltshire

PRELUDE TO LOVE

CHAPTER ONE

In June the Gallery filled up with tourists, visitors to the Lake District. The Reed Gallery was becoming well known among the discerning public.

'That guy has been here every afternoon for the last week.' Jenna Reed manoeuvred her wheelchair into a better position to survey the thinning crowds.

'Which guy?' I said, but I knew very well, because I too had observed his frequent visits.

'French, I think, or maybe Italian,' Jenna said consideringly. 'I want to see the colour of his eyes.'

'Now is the moment,' I said, as he approached the short counter behind which both Jenna and I were stationed.

'I am interested in the picture numbered thirty-two, by Felice Flyte. It is a genuine Flyte, I presume?' His voice had a slight inflection, which I thought was probably French. His eyes were dark, almost black, deep-set beneath straight eyebrows.

'Of course it is genuine. If we sell copies or prints we clearly mark them that way.' My voice sounded abrupt; it had been a long hard day.

He nodded. 'I thought so. Her work is unmistakable. Will you accept a deposit?'

1

He took a wallet from his jacket pocket and thrust a bunch of fivers into my hand. I counted them carefully, aware of his intent look which persisted until I gave him a receipt.

Then he smiled. 'Good. It is a beautiful picture.'

Jenna Reed wheeled herself nearer. His gaze rested on her face a moment, and then slid away. I could not be sure, but I thought his expression changed to pity; and that Jenna would not tolerate.

Hastily I said, 'I'll have it packed ready for collection.'

'Thank you. I will call early next week.'

'May I have your name?' I asked, with pen poised.

He hesitated, and then finally shrugged his shoulders. 'It is not important. Have no fear, I will return.'

He walked jauntily to the doors, and out into the street.

Jenna drew a noisy breath. 'Why didn't you insist on him giving his name, Lindsay? I want to know.'

'Too bad. He obviously wishes to remain anonymous.'

She hammered the arms of her chair with closed fists. 'Why do you always ignore me? I hate this place, Lindsay Strong.'

'If you hate it so much, why come? You don't have to; you are free to stay away.'

'I watch you. Roger expects me to do that.'

2

Her brilliant eyes were granite hard like some uncut jewel, an amethyst perhaps. She was strikingly beautiful, except for the discontented downturn of her mouth.

'Don't tell lies, Jen. Roger wouldn't dream of not trusting me.'

'Oh trust,' she said. 'You are so stupid. I know you don't want me on your patch.' Her voice was rising and I looked round, fearing the customers were near enough to hear this bitter exchange.

Davies was however shepherding the stragglers out. He was a stickler for time, and closed the Gallery exactly at the advertised hour.

'You are entitled to be here,' I said acidly, 'but you upset the staff with your ridiculous accusations. I shall speak to Roger ...'

'Speak to him! Go on! My brother won't take your side. He daren't.'

'What are you talking about?'

She smiled. 'I know too much.'

I turned away and began to check the till. Davies came back.

'Shall I help you down the step Miss Reed?'

'You mind your own business.'

He stood there, stolidly. Ex-Marine, broad-shouldered, deep-tanned, blue eyes inscrutable.

I turned back to Jenna. 'For God's sake, go. I've had as much of you today as I can take.'

'You don't care—no one does.'

3

Davies moved to the back of her chair and pushed it down the Gallery. 'I'll get even with you,' she screamed.

I sat down, breathing deeply, subduing the anger she aroused in me.

'Take no notice of her, Miss Lindsay.' Davies marched back up the Gallery. 'She finds it hard to live with guilt.'

Startled I looked at him. 'Guilt? I don't understand.'

'Best forget I said that. Are you ready?'

He accompanied me to the safe in the office, waiting while I deposited the day's takings. I felt comforted; there was an enormous strength in Davies.

'I'll put that picture in the stockroom,' he said, slapping a red sold ticket on the frame. 'A beauty.' He observed it closely. 'One of Her best.'

He always referred to my mother as 'Her' as if she was the only woman in the world for him. Maybe she was. Davies was a secretive man.

He carried the picture carefully as if it were made of solid gold. Together we locked up and left the Gallery.

*　　*　　*

The Gallery is on the waterfront, facing the steamer terminus. It is shaped like a cross, to the right is the bookshop, stocking all the Lakeland poets and writers. To the left is the

4

craft shop in which local crafts are sold. Both these departments are connected to the Gallery.

The streets of the town are terminated by the lake; spread fan-wise, upwards from the water. They are nevertheless, dominated by the lake's length, breadth and beauty.

The Gallery is a landmark in a way, a thriving memorial to Joshua Reed, who conceived the idea, built it, and dying, left it in the hands of his only son Roger, who has taken it for his own.

I began work at the Gallery by chance. My two years at a business school in London paid off. My first job was with a wine importer and I travelled widely with him. When my father was accidentally killed three years ago, I came home—to stay. Mother was devastated; she declared she could not live without my father, but her creative force was a burning necessity, and she was producing pictures of exquisite quality.

How could I leave her? She needed me desperately in the moments when she sat listlessly between pictures; and walking on the fells without seeming to know where she was, she frightened me.

Often, I followed her. She knew I was there trailing in the rear, but she gave no indication she was pleased; once only, she stopped, and waiting for me gathered me into her arms. Her tears wet my face, and the bond which had

5

always held us close, tightened.

The Reeds, particularly Roger, have always been friends. His father was the first to recognise my mother's talent. When first she arrived in the town as a young student, she signed her pictures with her maiden name of Felice Flyte, and continued to do so. Her pictures have been a feature of the Gallery for nearly thirty years.

Felice Flyte pictures have become very collectable, and she had already sold a number of canvases before she met and married my father, Coniston Strong. Her marriage in no way interfered with her art, and together they set up home in Fell Cottage, where she and I still live.

Situated a few miles from Longmere it overlooks an absolute gem of a lake. Sweetwater is small, with sharply rising fells on three sides. On the west shore the land is comparatively flat and a number of select residences are built near the water's edge.

As long as I can remember our cottage has been a gathering place for visiting artists, plus a coterie of rock climbers, great admirers of my father's skills. Coniston Strong's name was a byword among the climbing fraternity. He had conquered every peak in the district, and at the time of his death was preparing to make an assault on Everest.

I thought about them both, driving home along the narrow roads, hating their reflected

6

glory. I wanted my own, passionately.

Felice was standing at the window, gazing up towards the line of mountains facing the cottage. As I entered the room, she screwed up a letter she was holding and threw it in the empty fireplace.

'Hullo darling,' she said. 'I've made supper.'

'Good. I'm hungry.'

'You always are. I don't know why you never put on weight. You're like I was twenty-five years ago,' she said wistfully.

'You haven't changed.' I put my arms round her waist and hugged her. I wish I'd inherited her baby-soft fair hair, and wide blue eyes. I favoured my father, square chin, high cheekbones, and brown-gold flecked eyes, a match to the auburn hair which curled uncurbed.

She'd set the table with delicate care. Like a still life, I thought, noting the colourful bowl of fruit and trails of ivy. We sat down to eat.

'Roger was here,' she said, helping herself to salad. 'He accused me of acting behind his back.'

'Have you?' I heaped up my plate with chicken and ham.

'No, Lindsay, I have not,' she said vehemently. 'It was over this chap ...' she hesitated. 'He asked Roger for my address and wrote a letter. He thinks I'm undervalued. I guess Roger doesn't like the idea of anyone else handling my pictures.'

'What have you done?' I asked nervously.

'Nothing, honestly. Would I? Without consulting you?' She began to eat quickly, and wouldn't meet my glance.

'What's his name?'

'I forget,' she said, and laughed. 'Roger was very angry. He doesn't own us,' she looked at me directly, 'unless you intend a closer relationship.'

I smiled, watching her eyes widen and sparkle. 'You don't catch me like that, my dear mother. Roger and I are friends and business colleagues.'

'I like Roger, even when he's angry. He's devoted to you.'

'So you say. I sold another of your pictures today to a very dishy young man. He appears to be a great fan of yours. He was quite lyrical about your work.'

She reached for the wine bottle and filled her glass carefully. She was always amazed at her popularity, and in a way, resented strangers buying her pictures. Perhaps she thought she was selling a part of herself.

'Jenna was furious because he wouldn't reveal his name. Jen is slowly driving me mad.'

'I don't want to talk about Jenna. I've been thinking, Lindsay, I ought not to encourage you to stay here. I know you like being at the Gallery, but we all use you. And underneath there is this unspent emotion.'

'I don't know what you mean. Where would

I go?'

'I thought Italy. Both of us.'

I exclaimed in amazement, 'Do you mean that?'

'No, of course I don't,' she snapped. 'But for your sake ...'

'Felice, I'm not your baby chick any longer. I can fend for myself.'

'Not against unseen forces; they are beating on our door.'

Felice is like this; she is in tune with a strange world of her own. She only paints on auspicious days. She walks on the fells at dawn and dusk, attended by Barney the dog, who adores her.

Sometimes I believe in her unseen forces. Not long after Coniston's death she painted a strange picture. It had such power in the shapes and colours, I hid it. I could not bear to look at it. Even now the thought disturbed me. I jumped up and collected the dirty plates, and taking them into the kitchen, returned with a crystal bowl of fresh fruit salad and a jug of cream.

'This man I was telling you about,' she helped herself to fruit salad, 'he telephoned. I asked him to lunch tomorrow. You'll be here, it's Sunday.'

It was so unlike mother actually to invite anyone to a meal, I moved Barney off the hearthrug and retrieved the letter. Smoothing it out I read: *I'm a fervent admirer of your work.*

9

I have connections in Paris and Rome and think you should be exhibited in other places. Perhaps we can meet? Yours sincerely, P. Deauville.

'Do you want to be exhibited on the Continent?' I asked.

Her eyes glittered. 'Yes, I do. Coniston thought I should widen my scope. He said my pictures weren't just pictorial representations, they are an act of faith. He said that capturing the enduring beauty of the landscape proclaimed there is some pattern to life.'

I hadn't known my father had felt like that, and yet now I see it fitted in with his own obsession.

'Well, I suppose we can easily get rid of him after lunch,' I said resignedly. 'What do you propose we eat.'

'No problem,' she said proudly. 'I fetched steak from the butchers, at least Dora did. And you can pick peas out of the garden, and we will have the Wensleydale cheese. You will cook, won't you, darling?'

Felice is a disaster in the kitchen. Coniston had cooked until I was old enough to take over. He'd always said he hadn't married Felice for her prowess in the kitchen, it had been her irresistible smile.

She smiled now. 'There'll be four of us for lunch. I invited Roger too.'

*   *   *

10

I do not like having my Sundays organised. I need my day of freedom to gear myself up for another week. Felice's luncheon party angered me. Once again, she was using me.

Felice's life is not governed by time, but by inclination and inspiration. This Sunday I woke her early with a glass of lemon tea.

'Darling, what do you want me to do? You manage so well. Perhaps I should tidy the studio?'

She wouldn't, of course. She would ignore all the preparations, and sail into the dining-room as if she had been the one slaving over a hot stove. The peas were ready for picking, but first I dug up a couple of roots of new potatoes. The garden cried out for attention. It was too long and too big, and only manageable because Con had planted the bottom end with firs, which he had intended selling for Christmas trees. Now the firs were over ten feet tall, and were shouldering their way determinedly beyond the confines of the garden and on to the fell.

'You're out early, Lindsay,' our next door neighbour, Dora Crumb called over the fence.

'Felice is having a lunch party.'

Dora joined me. 'Well, well! Who?' She had been widowed about twenty years ago, and was sorrowing still not for her husband but her son who had walked out early one morning and worked a passage on a ship to Canada, and had never returned. She was plump with

11

sparkling blue eyes, and an infectious laugh. She loved my mother.

'Roger, and some guy who admires her art.'

Dora bent down, picking peas. 'Roger won't like that.'

'Roger will have to lump it.'

Dora laughed. 'You'll lose that fellow one day.'

'I don't own him, so how can I lose him?'

'I presume Jenna isn't invited.'

I straightened up, and shaking my head, led the way to the kitchen. Dora followed.

'Is Felice still in one of her helpless moods? Shall I run her bath?' She whisked upstairs. She was indispensable, but Felice would never acknowledge it, and used her shamefully; as she does us all, I thought.

Roger arrived early, walking in through the open front door.

'Lindsay!'

'Here.' He followed the sound of my voice to the kitchen, and coming up behind, hugged me and planted a gentle kiss on my cheek. He has a restful kind of face, even features, and a full mouth.

'Good trip?' I asked. He launched into a description of his business deals in London, waving the bunch of roses he carried to their danger.

'For Felice—a peace offering.' He grinned. 'We had a difference of opinion.'

'So I heard.'

12

'What's she up to Lindsay? I thought she was satisfied with the way we handle her pictures. Why this sudden change of heart?'

'I don't know. Who is this P. Deauville?'

'I intend to find out,' Roger said grimly.

'She's invited the man to lunch.'

Roger laughed. 'Good.'

'It might be to her advantage,' I said nervously.

'We'll see.' He rearranged the roses and went through to the sitting-room. Dora came in for a vase, and winked. 'They are flattering each other.'

'A bad sign,' I said, scraping the potatoes.

The telephone rang and I called to Roger to take the call. He summoned me peremptorily. 'It's Deauville,' he said.

I took the receiver from his hand.

'Miss Flyte?'

'No. This is her daughter.'

'I am so sorry I can't make lunch today. May I postpone my visit?'

'Certainly. We'll be pleased to see you another day.'

'You will apologise to your mother. I am deeply disappointed.'

'And so are we,' I said politely.

I cradled the receiver and paused for thought, glancing at the time. An hour before lunch seemed like short notice. Still, he had sounded agitated; maybe he'd suddenly got cold feet.

I put my head round the sitting-room door. 'That was Deauville. He isn't coming. He's very sorry Felice. Hopes you'll invite him another time.'

Felice looked at Roger. 'This is your doing. How dare you interfere?'

'Hold on, Felice. I have nothing to do with it, I swear.'

'Then who?' Her gaze fell on me. 'It's a conspiracy between you.'

'Don't be ridiculous, Mother. You are being dramatic. People often cancel at the last moment. Perhaps he's feeling ill.'

'Oh the poor man.' She was suddenly all heart. 'I'll write him a note, and you, Roger, can deliver it to the Lake End Hotel.'

'After lunch?' he queried.

She was herself again. 'Of course, dear Roger. Would I deprive you of lunch or Lindsay's company?'

I returned to the kitchen and in a moment Roger followed.

'What happened?' he asked.

'I don't know. Do you?' I faced him. 'Are you taking lessons from Jenna?'

He grabbed me by the shoulders. 'What do you mean?'

'I mean she will do anything to get her own way, and it seems you are determined this man shouldn't meet Felice. I can't stand much more of your sister, and unless you keep her out of the Gallery, I'm resigning.'

14

He stared at me aghast. 'But you can't Lindsay. I can't manage without you. I know Jenna is difficult—but the poor girl ...'

'Roger, did she ever tell you the truth about the accident.'

'I don't understand. Of course she did.'

'I know the official story. My father and Jenna tackled High Sail. They both fell. I don't know why or how. Felice believes it was Jenna's fault. She has absolute faith in Con's record as a climber, and nothing is going to change her mind.'

'I don't think Jenna was to blame.' He paused and sighed. 'She won't talk about it. I think she doesn't remember what happened. She was unconscious when they were rescued, and remained so for several days. Please don't let this come between us.' He took hold of my hands. 'I need you Lindsay. I won't let you mention leaving.'

Felice came to the door. 'What are you two whispering about?'

'Nothing, darling,' I soothed. 'Let's have lunch. And afterwards we can take Barney a walk on the fells.'

'Count me out,' Felice said. 'I have a picture to finish. You two go. I'm sure you have lots of business to discuss—like conspiracy.'

15

CHAPTER TWO

Deauville telephoned in the afternoon three days later. Felice didn't tell me until we were drinking coffee after dinner.

Casually she said, 'Mr Deauville phoned. I invited him round for a drink tomorrow evening. Do get home early, darling.'

Roger was in Amsterdam on the trail of a particular picture which a customer had commissioned him to buy. Before leaving, he had acted as peacemaker between Jenna and myself, and reluctantly I agreed to keep her occupied at the Gallery during the daytime.

'She's lonely,' he said.

Miss Linton, the Reeds' elderly nurse-housekeeper, hadn't the same tastes as Jenna, which didn't surprise me in the least. Jen adored pop music and was the third player in a three piece band. She played the guitar brilliantly.

Jenna arrived at the Gallery much subdued. It was a temporary phase, but one of which to take advantage. And as a penance she undertook to do some of the filing in the office. During the afternoon I had to go out, and when I returned, she was radiant.

'He's been back,' she greeted me. 'You know,' she continued as I looked at her blankly, 'the mystery guy who bought one of

Felice's pictures. He said he'd collect it at the end of the week.'

'Did you get his name?' Was I being spiteful?

She looked crestfallen. 'No. But I will find out who he is.'

The mysterious young man was not in my mind at this moment, but Mr P. Deauville was. I was afraid mother would get entangled with him.

Felice phoned during the afternoon to remind me to leave early, and when I walked in at the door she was dressed for the part of a successful artist. She acts almost as well as she paints, and fancies herself a second Sarah Bernhardt. She wore a flimsy dress, in shades of grey and lemon, and a long string of opal beads round her neck. It was her idea of how an artist should look.

Dora Crumb cooked dinner and sat down to enjoy it with us. I was grateful for her help, often feeling jaded when I returned late from the Gallery.

'What time is this exciting man coming?' she asked archly. 'Do you think I could have a peep at him?'

'Of course. You must stay and have a drink with us.' I thought if Dora was there, Felice wouldn't commit herself to any kind of agreement.

'Felice says you don't approve of him. I think she deserves to be better known.'

'Of course she does. But believe me, it is the

quality of her work which will build up her reputation, not strange men flattering her with vague suggestions. I distrust them,' I added.

Dora clamped her full lips together. 'I'm sure you'll do what's best for Felice,' she said primly as the front doorbell pealed.

I opened the door and was face to face with the mysterious young man who so intrigued Jenna.

'Hallo,' the inflection in his voice was less pronounced. 'This is a surprise. You can't be Felice Flyte?'

He sounded so incredulous that I replied sharply, 'No, I am not. She isn't at home.'

'There must be some mistake. She invited me. I'm Philippe Deauville.'

Slightly stunned by this revelation I invited him in.

'Mr Deauville,' I announced.

Felice fluttered to her feet, and placed her hand in his outstretched one. She appeared to be struck by his looks, because it was several moments before she said, 'May I introduce you to my daughter, Lindsay, and our friend Mrs Crumb.'

He withdrew his hand from Felice's grasp and offered it to Dora. She was gazing at him with a slightly puzzled expression.

'Your daughter and I have already met,' he smiled at Felice.

'You didn't tell me Lindsay.' Felice was annoyed.

'I didn't know who he was. He came into the Gallery to buy one of your pictures. Do sit down, Mr Deauville.'

I indicated a chair facing the settee on which Felice now sank, spreading her skirt carefully round her. On his entry into the room he had put a bottle on the table. He now picked it up and offered it to Felice.

'Will you forgive me bringing a bottle of wine, but this is a special occasion for me. And this champagne is kind of special too.'

'How lovely,' she said. 'Lindsay, fetch the champagne glasses. I love special occasions.'

How true, I thought. There had been a time when she had made life itself special; when she and Coniston had such a largess of happiness, it had encompassed me too.

I fetched the glasses, and he opened the bottle and poured the wine, offering a glass to each of us. Then he sat down, leaning back in the chair, smiling, perfectly at ease.

He tasted the wine and nodded. 'A good year,' he said. 'I must explain there is a small vineyard on the Deauville estate which is luckily in the Champagne district.'

Felice seemed to lose her reservation. 'How exciting. Are you here on holiday? I presume you live in France.'

He shook his head, and turned to me. 'What do you think of the wine?'

'Excellent, Mr Deauville.'

'Please. Call me Philippe. I hate formality.'

19

I sipped the champagne, and thought he was a fast mover. There wasn't any doubt about his attractiveness. Dora was practically open-mouthed.

'And how do vineyards and pictures match up?' I asked. 'Or am I to presume you are a collector and not a dealer.'

'Dealer!' He looked at me as if I'd uttered a dirty word. 'No. I do not deal in pictures. I have long wanted to meet Felice Flyte. You see, my mother brought two of your pictures with her from England,' he said, smiling at her.

Felice was enthralled. 'Did she buy them on holiday?'

'No. My mother was English. She died a year ago, and left me these two pictures. Since then my father has also died.'

'Oh dear,' Felice said. 'How sad. I am so sorry.'

'He will be greatly missed.' He jumped up and asked permission to fetch another bottle from the car.

'He's charming,' Dora gushed. The wine had brightened her cheeks to a cherry. Her happiness in participating in our lives which she considered artistic and exciting was palpable.

'He's suave, and I'd like to know his game,' I said.

'Game!' Felice and Dora spoke simultaneously in scandalised tones.

'I don't understand,' Dora continued

20

weakly. 'Surely you don't think ...'

I was thinking a lot of things, and none of them complimentary to Philippe Deauville. However, as the evening progressed, and Felice became more withdrawn, I began to think I needn't worry.

Eventually he turned his attention to me. His enquiries about the Reed Gallery were surprisingly informed.

'I understand Mr Reed buys the pictures. Is he an expert?'

'Expert at what? Picking winners, do you mean; or has he a nose for buying pictures that sell?'

Philippe's well-defined brows drew together in a frown. 'But that's business.'

'Certainly. He runs the Gallery very successfully.'

'Roger would be helpless without Lindsay,' Dora said.

'Rubbish, Dora. I do my job well, that's all.'

Philippe leaned forward as if to focus my complete attention. 'I thought, perhaps, you were a partner ...?' he paused enquiringly.

'Why should you think that? I don't look for trouble.'

He laughed. 'Maybe you are the power behind the throne. It would be a pity to waste your talents.'

'What talent I have isn't wasted. And I don't see ...'

'You're right,' he said cheerfully, 'it isn't any

21

of my business.'

Felice stood up. She cannot bear not to be the centre of attention. 'Lindsay hasn't any ambition,' she said disparagingly.

'I don't think that's true,' he said gently, and stood up. 'Perhaps you would show me your studio another day. I do hope I haven't outstayed my welcome.'

He glanced at me, but I didn't answer. I had not welcomed him, and now wanted him gone. His presence disturbed me in a way no other man's had ever done.

He invited the three of us to lunch at the Lake End Hotel on Sunday. Felice and Dora accepted, but I made excuses. I would let him know, but I was prevaricating, because I thought it would be fatal to let Felice loose alone with him. And until I knew what he wanted, I had to guard her interests.

*   *   *

I didn't mention my meeting with Deauville to the Reeds, as it was no concern of theirs, and I preferred to handle the man myself. But he had struck a faint chord in my mind. I began to wonder if I had indeed subconsciously resented a subordinate position.

I observed with newly-opened eyes. Much of the success of the Gallery was mine. Did Roger know? I discounted Jenna, but it was she who put slightly more substance to my thoughts.

Our truce had only lasted three days until Roger's return.

'You act as if you own the place,' she said irritably.

Her outburst was due to the fact I'd asked Davies to construct a new background for the window. Jenna had organised the swathes of material which were now dusty and faded, and I was sure a more permanent affair would be better.

Davies had a hobby, woodwork. He'd learnt in his youth, and had picked up a collection of carved animals from many of the ports he'd visited. He delighted in constructing realistic backgrounds for these animals, and occasionally Roger allowed him to display them.

Roger, for once, sided with me. And Jenna sulked. Davies, aware of the tension between us, made the kind of background I'd in mind. It was a series of slanted boards, on which pictures could be easily hung, and he and I fitted it when Roger had taken Jenna to the hospital for a check-up.

Deauville came in for his picture that afternoon. He paid the balance in cash, and invited me to have dinner with him that evening. I hesitated, and he laid a hand lightly on my arm. 'Please do, Lindsay. I'm not sure how much longer I shall stay here, and I enjoy your company.'

It sounded innocuous enough. Dinner and

conversation might enable me to discover what his object was. I agreed, and he was waiting outside the Gallery in his car when Davies and I closed up the place. He drove to the Lake End Hotel with a French disregard for other traffic. Thankfully I alighted and he suggested a drink in the cocktail bar.

'Awful place.' He found us a table near the window, which overlooked a tired lawn, and the lake.

I agreed. It had only recently been added to the hotel, and was totally out of keeping with the rest of the building which had originally been a drover's stopping place.

'I like this town, the lake and the mountains, especially the mountains.' He paused while our drinks were served. 'Do you climb?'

'Not now.'

'A pity. I was hoping you would act as guide. Felice says you walk miles on the fells.'

'When did she tell you that?' I asked sharply.

'She phoned and invited me to see her studio. I guess you didn't want me to see her alone. You think I have an ulterior motive in talking to her.' He laughed. 'I have in a way ...'

'Your letter implied your interest wasn't just personal.'

'It's true I have connections—family connections—in Europe. My brothers own a splendid Gallery in Paris. They are keen on English regional painters. Your mother has a great deal of ambition. And I'm sure she didn't

24

speak the truth when she said you had none.'

I shrugged. I had no intention of discussing my ambition or lack of it. But my curiosity was aroused. We had a couple more drinks, and then moved into the dining-room. He consulted me minutely on the menu and wine. I felt special, as if he really cared I had a free choice. Not like Roger, I thought ruefully. He always ordered, and if I demurred, he always said he knew what I liked, and made me feel as if we were an old married couple.

In spite of my reservations I began to enjoy his company. Coffee was served in the lounge, and when we were comfortably seated, he said, 'I showed Felice my two pictures. She didn't remember painting them.'

'Are you sure?'

He nodded. 'I think if her signature wasn't on the canvas, she'd have denied ever seeing them before. You see, I'm interested in the location. In fact I'm determined to track it down. She said you might recognise it.'

There was an intensity in his manner which made it seem important. I began to think this was the object of the dinner, especially when he asked me if I'd go to his room to look at the pictures.

His room overlooked the lake. There was a desk and several comfortable chairs. He unlocked the wardrobe and lifted out the pictures. They were quite small and framed in plain wood. He turned on a bright desk lamp,

25

and I held them in turn under the strong light.

'Did she paint them?' he asked urgently.

'They are certainly signed by her, so she must have done.' I marvelled at the maturity of her early work. 'Anyway, I doubt if they are copies.'

'I don't care if they are copies. All I want to know is the location.'

I studied them closely. Both pictures were of the same view, only a strange lapse of time seemed to have taken place. The first was of a house vaguely outlined against a background of fells, and in the foreground there was an ornamental lake. The second picture was much more interesting. The house now appeared as a ruin, and the fells had turned into the familiar shape of a mountain I could never forget. The ornamental lake had vanished, and its place was taken by two figures standing facing the house. The man's arm was round the woman's shoulders as if to comfort her.

'She must remember,' I said. 'Perhaps she doesn't want to,' I added thoughtfully. 'Who do you suppose those figures represent?'

'I don't know. My mother never explained. And in any case she didn't show them to me until she was dying.'

'Didn't your father recognise them?'

'He never came to England. I was educated here, but it was always mother who came to school events, and later to University when I graduated.' He hesitated and looked away. 'I haven't lived in France for some time. I teach at Blairgow School.' He named a well-known private school. 'My brothers were educated in France.'

His diffidence was intriguing, and I too, began to wonder why his mother had kept her past secret.

'If your mother has second thoughts, or maybe you can jog her memory, I'd be eternally grateful,' he said, as we returned to the lounge for more coffee.

And suddenly we were chatting like old friends. He had been teaching French at Blairgow for five years, and enjoyed his job.

'Especially cricket. I coach the second team, and we have more wins than the first. But my real love is art. I paint in oils, but not with much success. My brothers are the critics.'

'Wouldn't you have preferred to establish yourself in the art world?'

'Once,' he said. 'Not now. The circumstances are changed. My mother insisted on my coming to England to teach. Do you paint?'

I laughed. 'No. I enjoy business. I had a super job with a wine importer before I came home and started work at the Gallery.' I glanced at my watch. 'Heavens, look at the time. I must be off.'

He offered to drive me home, but I needed my car for the morning. He held my hand in parting, and thanked me for my kindness.

Actually I thought it was he who had been so attentive as to make the evening such a pleasant one.

I let myself into the cottage, and Barney came bounding out of the kitchen. Felice was in her room with the door shut, and I followed Barney out into the garden. He loped away to the Christmas tree plantation, ever hopeful of raising a rabbit or two.

Philippe Deauville's second picture had deeply disturbed me. Outside in the cool night, looking up at the diadem of stars circling the highest fells I felt a shiver of apprehension.

Why had Felice painted that particular mountain so long ago, and why did she deny all memory of it?

Barney came racing back, and I followed him into the cottage and locked up. Felice was standing on the landing, and called down.

'I long for a cup of tea,' she said. 'I can't sleep.'

I took the tray up to her and poured out for both of us and sat down on the bed. She was propped up against her pillows, and with a jolt I noticed the lines round her mouth and at the corners of her eyes.

'You're late,' she said irritably. 'I worry. Roger is very thoughtless.'

'Roger! I haven't seen Roger. I had dinner with Philippe Deauville.'

Her voice hardened. 'Why?'

'It was a spur of the moment invitation. He

came to collect his picture, and asked me to relieve his loneliness,' I said lightly.

'And did you?' She was not joking.

'It depends what you mean.' I looked her straight in the eyes. She held out her cup and I refilled it. 'Felice, why did you tell Philippe you don't remember painting his two pictures?'

'Is he still harping on that subject? I painted lots of pictures when I first came here before I married Con. They were bought by old Mr Reed. Perhaps those were among them.'

'Very likely. But why that particular mountain?'

She shivered, but I persisted. 'And that house? Had it any significance for you? It also seems to disturb Philippe.'

'I don't remember any house, and the mountain is just a mountain, and God knows there are enough of them. And the figures are out of my imagination. Does that satisfy you?'

'I suppose so,' I said grudgingly. 'Let's forget it.'

'You won't,' she said sombrely. 'Not while he's here. Ask him to go away, Lindsay. He's a danger to us.'

CHAPTER THREE

Felice's changed attitude to Philippe Deauville puzzled me. She phoned him at the hotel and cancelled Sunday lunch. Dora was not consulted.

Philippe was waiting outside the Gallery the next evening. The Reeds left early, and it was well past closing-time before I was ready to leave. Davies always waited for me, and together we locked up and set the burglar alarm.

Philippe was in the car-park, leaning against the bonnet of my car.

'You look tired,' he stated. 'How about a drink?'

'A cup of coffee would be fine, but I mustn't hang about. Mother is expecting some friends.'

He took my arm, and we walked to the newly-opened coffee shop further along the waterfront.

'Your mother phoned,' he said. 'She's changed her mind about having lunch on Sunday. Why?'

'She's unpredictable.'

'Have I offended her, Lindsay?'

'Troubled her, perhaps. For some reason she doesn't want to be reminded of the paintings you showed her.'

'Because it's her early work, would you say?'

'I don't know. She may feel dissatisfied with them.'

'I can understand that. Perhaps when I get back from London on Saturday, I could talk to her. Lindsay, will you spend Sunday with me? I thought we might walk on the fells.' He hesitated, and then said in a rush, 'The mountain in my picture has been identified.'

'Really!'

'I think you recognised it. But I see you don't want to be involved.'

'What is this? Involved in what? I'm perfectly willing to go walking on Sunday and hunt for this mythical house.'

His eyes sparkled and he took my hand. 'You mean it, Lindsay? You don't mind giving up your free day to be with me?'

'I shall enjoy it. It's more fun to walk with a companion, and Felice soon gets tired and bored.'

'I thought perhaps Mr Reed ...?'

'Roger! No, he exhausts himself playing squash, and in any case we see enough of each other without meeting on Sundays.'

I didn't mention my plans for Sunday to Felice, knowing she would think I was going somewhere with Roger. This was the first time I'd been secretive; in fact my life was so open and accounted for, I had a need to have unshared hours. This was my chance.

Jenna was still angry over the fact her mysterious man had collected his picture while she wasn't in the Gallery. I didn't enlighten her as to his identity, nor did I mention to Roger I'd had any further contact with 'that fellow'.

It seemed Roger had lost interest in Philippe Deauville, some greater worry making him quiet and morose.

'What's the matter, Roger?' I asked as we sat over a lunch-time drink and sandwich in the bar in the Lake End Hotel.

'Nothing. Nothing at all.'

'Is it Jen?' I persisted. 'Is something wrong in the Gallery?'

'I tell you there's nothing to worry you about,' he said irritably.

'So there is something.' I realised how well I knew Roger. Not just his moods—he didn't have many of those—but I had come to understand how his mind worked.

I returned to the subject of Jenna. 'Is she playing you up?'

'No more than usual. She is a trial. Some days . . .' he paused.

'So if it isn't Jen, it's business. Unless you've fallen in love?' I added lightly, and wasn't prepared for his angry rejoinder.

'Don't be a damn fool. There's only one woman in the world for me. You.' He reached for my hand, holding it tightly. He's like a man drowning in a dark sea, I thought, and I am the spar to which he clings.

'So,' I gently withdrew my hand, 'it's business. Money?'

'You know from the books we have a substantial bank balance.'

'I don't get it,' I said impatiently, and stood up. 'I must go. Are you coming back to the Gallery now?'

'Later. I have to see a bloke.'

I tried to get this teasing conversation out of mind, but at odd intervals it returned to puzzle me. Davies was in the office when I returned, and I sent him off to lunch, and took the books out of the safe.

Had Roger found some discrepancy in the accounting? I checked the figures carefully. The weekly takings were rising sharply as we advanced into the season. I couldn't find the smallest mistake.

On Davies's return, we went into the stockroom. This was a dark room, the only window high up, small and barred. Davies turned on the fluorescent lights by the door into the office. There was also an outer door which opened on to a narrow alley-way, and was a convenient loading bay. This door was always kept locked when not in use, and the two-way switch for the lights, and the burglar alarm were both conveniently within reach.

Pictures were selling well, and I made a careful choice of replacements. Roger never interfered in the picture hanging, but Jenna did. She disputed my choice continuously.

On this afternoon she followed us around as we rearranged the display.

'It isn't fair.' She wheeled herself in front of the permanent display of Felice's pictures. 'Why should she have all that space?'

Davies in close attendance, stiffened, but he didn't speak.

'Your father made that arrangement with

her,' I said.

'Well, he's dead,' she said brutally. 'And Roger and I are the bosses. And I say we want a change. Davies, take the Flyte pictures to the stockroom.'

Davies didn't move. He stood ramrod straight, arms clamped to his side.

'Do you hear me?' her voice rose.

'I hear you, but I don't touch them unless Mr Roger says so.'

At that moment Roger entered the Gallery. 'Come here,' she called.

'What's the problem?'

Jenna said, 'I want space taken up by the Flyte pictures to display John Ritter's canvases.'

So that was it. Ritter is a local artist, and I'd noticed him deep in conversation with Jenna one day, and no doubt they'd set up a deal.

'Davies refused to move them,' she said.

'I take my instructions from you Mr Reed. But in my opinion most of the customers only come to see her pictures.'

'You're besotted with her.' Jenna was furious. 'You'd think she was a goddess the way you worship her.'

Davies's expression changed; for the first time in our long acquaintance Jenna had got under his skin. His face whitened.

'If her pictures are removed, I shall hand in my notice.'

'This is ridiculous.' Roger's anger never

34

spurted out, it was contained, and all the more dangerous. 'The Flyte pictures stay where they are, and what's more, I've arranged with Felice for a special showing. Lindsay, I'd like to discuss dates with you.'

'Roger, you're as besotted with her as him.' She pointed to Davies.

'That's enough, Jen.' Roger pushed her chair towards the doors. 'If you can't behave responsibly, please go home.'

*　　*　　*

On Sunday the sun rose in an amethyst sky. The early light was amber, and flooded my room as I dressed. A quick breakfast, and I was ready. Felice still slept, and Dora was leaning out of her window as I stepped outside.

'A day out?' she queried, noting my walking gear. 'Do you good, love. Is Felice awake?'

'Not yet.'

'Don't you worry. I'll go in and keep her company.'

Philippe was waiting. Barney belted up to him, and after a few preliminary sniffs, accepted him.

'I was afraid you wouldn't come. I thought you'd think me crazy. This mythical house,' he shrugged, 'there are so many places it could be.'

'I've studied the map, Philippe. I've got a few ideas.'

35

We fell into step, and began the ascent which would bring us along the top of Gorton Fell.

The sky deepened to a depthless blue, reflected in the lake below us. The sunshine had paled to a softer yellow, and cast black shadows where the rocks faced away from it.

We were ahead of the other walkers, and I revelled in the speaking silence, broken only by the distant bleat of a sheep, and the eerie call of the curlew.

'I have a strange feeling of familiarity,' Philippe said. 'I think my mother told me stories about the mountains.'

'Was her home here?'

He shrugged. 'I don't think so. When she married she took French nationality. My father called her Yvette, but her English name was Eve.'

We climbed steadily. I had discovered the perfect walking companion. No senseless chatter, just a feeling that we saw the folds of the hills, the glint of water, the widening landscape with the same eyes.

We traversed the long line of Gorton Fell and dropped down into the valley where the compact stone houses of Mosthwaite clustered round the pub. It was now nearly midday, and we entered the low raftered saloon bar. Philippe ordered drinks and sandwiches, and the landlord suggested we ate outside. 'Make the most of the day,' he stroked his bearded chin, 'for weather will surely change.'

'How can he know?' Philippe sat down and gazed at the brilliant sky.

'See that cloud, sitting on top of High Sail? By the time we've eaten our lunch it will have billowed out and obscured the sun.'

'It is the right mountain, isn't it?'

I forced myself to notice every detail in the translucent air. It was the mountain Felice had painted in Philippe's picture; the mountain I had avoided for three years, the mountain on which my father had died.

I had so often wondered about that accident. Why had my father, who was a superb climber been killed, and Jenna, a novice, injured? I forced myself to look at the treacherous north face. Two tiny figures, no larger than flies, were clinging to the surface. I shivered and turned my head away, covering my face with my hands.

'Lindsay, are you all right?' Philippe scraped his chair along the paving stones to my side. He was so close, his arm tentatively round my shoulders.

'I'm OK. You see, it was on that mountain that my father was killed.'

'Oh God, what have I done? To hurt you like this.'

'No, Philippe, it is better I came here with you. A stranger, not knowing, not caring ...'

He stopped me, with a finger on my lips. 'I care, oh yes, dear Lindsay, I care. But I don't understand. Why did Felice paint this

37

particular mountain, and a beautiful house suddenly ruined, and those two people all those years ago?'

'I don't know. Perhaps a time slip. A foreknowledge that High Sail would spell disaster for her, as it has for so many others.'

'And the house?'

'Why is it important to you?' I countered with another question.

'I think my mother knew it,' he said simply.

'Why do you think this is so special?'

'I feel it.'

We finished our drinks and sandwiches, and as forecast the clouds were banking up and slithering down High Sail's jagged rocks. I unfolded the map and pointed out a small dot on the southern slope.

'There must be a building of some sort there. If we take a direct route round the base of High Sail, we should reach it before the rain. And if the weather really closes in we can return by road.'

'Perhaps we should start back now?'

'Certainly not. We've come so far, we must go on.'

We struck out along the floor of the valley. If it rained heavily, it would become a bog, running with a thousand streamlets. Philippe took my hand. I don't know if it comforted him, but it certainly comforted me. His hand was narrow, long fingered, and he wore a thin gold ring on his little finger.

In a short while we came to a narrow path, and looking at the map it appeared to be a track directly to the building. Walking on this was easier. I was surprised to note it appeared to be well used, until I realised it wound beyond the building and up part of the south side of the mountain.

We came on the building suddenly. No way could it have ever been Felice's dream house. It was built of Cumberland stone, the lower room still intact, but the ladder to the upper room had long since gone. From the amount of litter I guessed it was used by climbers and walkers as a shelter.

Philippe leaned against the lintel. 'It would have been too easy ...'

'Yes,' I said. 'Too easy.' I don't think I believed in the reality of the house, but I was puzzled by Philippe's obsession, for such it seemed, to track it down.

'We've only just started looking. Is it so important to you?'

He nodded. 'Why else did she, my mother, buy those pictures. They must have had meaning for her.'

'People buy pictures for all sorts of reasons. Mostly because they like the look of them.'

'That's right. And they hang them on their walls, and proudly inform their friends they have bought a bargain or it's some secret place.'

'Secret place, Philippe? Why should you

think that?'

'She didn't hang either of those pictures on her wall. She kept them hidden, locked up, and only when she knew she was dying did she ask me to look after them.'

I understood the importance Philippe attached to his mother's dying wish. Perhaps this place had meant something to her. But his obsession seemed to be out of all proportion.

'Let's go,' I said. And that moment the rain started. It lashed down, and thunder, which had been rumbling in the distance, crashed overhead. Lightning severed the sky, and poor Barney whimpered and crouched down in the corner. I pulled his trembling body close, and buried my head in his fur. He wasn't the only one scared. Philippe hadn't moved. He was smiling.

'Isn't it wonderful, Lindsay. Elemental, exciting, it sends my pulses racing.'

'You're welcome,' I muttered.

He turned his shining face to where I crouched in the dark.

'You're not scared, surely?'

'Yes, I am,' I said defiantly. 'I always have been.'

He was across the room in two strides, and raising me up put his arms round me and I hid my face against his chest.

'While I am here,' he said, 'you never need be afraid of anything. I promise.'

An easy promise, I thought. In a few weeks

he'd be gone. A new term at Blairgow School. Back, perhaps, to some woman; wife, fiancée, friend. And my whole being revolted against the thought.

He lifted my chin and looked deep into my eyes. What was he trying to tell me? A vivid blue flash lit up the dingy room, a flash which changed his face into some frightening mask, and then he bent his head, and his mouth fastened on mine, and I was lost.

One kiss, that was all. He lifted his head, and loosened his hold.

'The storm is passing. Shall we go now?' he said.

I nodded agreement. But the storm had not passed for me. Philippe Deauville had stirred in me a storm which might never pass.

CHAPTER FOUR

Felice didn't want a special exhibition of her pictures at the Gallery, or so she said. I waited, watching for the signs she was changing her mind, or rather, playing hard to get.

'I could have an exhibition in London or Paris,' she said.

'Go ahead.'

'You don't believe me. Just because I keep Reed's rotten old Gallery supplied with pictures, you think no one else wants them.'

'Who does?'

She faltered, and her eyes became misty blue with unshed tears. 'You've changed, Lindsay, ever since that awful Frenchman came here.'

Surprised I glared at her. 'I don't know what you mean.'

'He's no good to you. I know that, and if you've any sense you'll keep out of his way.'

Next day she capitulated. 'You can exhibit my work,' she said, 'but if you wish me to attend the opening make sure Jenna isn't there.'

I relayed the good news to Roger, but not the rider. I'd cope with that somehow when the time came.

The next few days were spent in an advertising campaign. The opening of the exhibition was always a big event in Longmere's calendar. This year, Roger had no heart for it. He hadn't recovered from his moroseness, and suggested I take charge of the arrangements.

I flung myself into the work with renewed energy.

Davies protested. 'Have sense, Miss Lindsay. There's plenty of time. No need to go over the top. We've never had a failure yet.'

The date set for the exhibition was the first two weeks in August. This was strategic, because it was then the whole area was saturated with visitors; and rain sent them scurrying into the town. It often rained during those two weeks.

'Why not take the exhibition to Paris?' Philippe asked. Habitually he was waiting for me when the Gallery closed. 'We could go over and talk to the right people.'

I shook my head. 'No time.'

He laughed. 'Are you afraid to spend a weekend with me?'

'Don't be silly, Philippe,' I said crossly. 'Now is not the time. I have responsibilities.'

'Too many, Lindsay. You give too much of yourself.'

We were strolling along the path by the lake, before we went to the hotel for a meal. The lake had a silver sheen, creased by the boats racing up and down. Hurrying waves responded to the disturbance, slapping and sucking against the bank.

'It's the only way I know.'

He nodded. 'That's how I was once. You give your all, and what happens? Circumstances change, and we ourselves are changed.'

'Felice says I've changed—for the worse. I can't be like Con was, a slave to her every whim.'

'You must never be overwhelmed by her personality. It is too fierce, too demanding.'

Philippe was the first person to realise the situation. Roger never mentioned it; perhaps it needed an outsider to see the reality. Nevertheless I felt a stab of disloyalty. I could criticise Felice, but I wasn't prepared to let anyone else.

As if sensing my slight displeasure he changed the subject. 'I've hired a boat for Sunday. I thought the three of us could picnic at the other end of the lake. Would you enjoy that?'

'Three?' I queried.

His delighted laugh rang out. Heads turned, and stayed turned.

'Surely you wouldn't want to leave Barney at home. What a dog! I am captivated by his ways.'

'Oh, Barney!' My heart sang with relief.

'I'm a tease,' he said. 'Will you come.'

* * *

The thought of our impending boat trip was like a child's special treasure. A leaf, a shell perhaps, some small thing to give pleasure. I thought about it in odd moments, which weren't many. I had a much more pressing worry. Roger.

Our warm comradeship was evaporating. He treated me as if I were just an employee, and although he consulted me on some matters, others which he had in the past left to me he now performed himself.

I suppose at the back of my mind I thought he disapproved of my flowering friendship with Philippe. But I didn't really think he was

44

aware of it, and indeed he seemed to have put Philippe completely out of his mind.

There was no one I could ask for help. No way of breaking through the barrier Roger was raising daily, and after a lot of hard thinking, I tried to pinpoint a moment when I'd noticed he didn't seem to trust me.

Jenna, I thought. And yet, what? She'd been trying to oust me from Roger's regard ever since I'd come to work at the Gallery. So why should he listen to her now? It was my inclination to tackle Roger outright, but he had gone away, and this time without telling me where I could get in touch with him.

I was deeply hurt. I was sure I was innocent of whatever crime Roger was holding me responsible for, and in the meantime I had plenty of work to do.

Davies had decided to reorganise the stockroom. It was his domain, and I had no objection.

'We are carrying a lot of stock which is sticking. I thought we could look through it,' he said diffidently.

I agreed. I'd noticed a number of what I termed Roger's 'bad buys' and suggested we put them on one side and ask Roger to dispose of them. It was no problem evaluating the framed pictures, but there were a number of canvases rolled and lodged on shelves. Among these were the John Ritter paintings which Jenna was so keen to have displayed.

'I suppose we should give them a short showing,' I said. 'How about frames?'

We kept a stock of frames, and Davies said he would fix them up if I chose the most likely to sell. I picked out a couple of charcoal drawings of the Langdales which struck me as compelling.

'How about this?' Davies held up a delicate pen and ink sketch, and I drew in my breath sharply.

'Is that one of Ritter's?' It was unsigned, but the resemblance to Philippe's picture of the house and mountain was so marked, I could hardly believe it.

Davies studied it critically. 'Too good for him,' he pronounced. 'I think it is one of Hers.'

'How did it get among these?' I said sharply.

Davies shrugged. 'Mr Reed was going through these canvases on Sunday. He asked me to give him a hand.'

'But he never looks at the canvases. Where are his latest purchases?'

Davies indicated a couple of rolled canvases. 'He has an idea there may be other paintings underneath.'

I studied them closely, but couldn't agree with Roger in this case.

'He said he'd have a go at restoring them when he has the time.' Davies gave me a hard look. 'He seems unsettled. Is something worrying him, Miss Lindsay? Can you talk to him?'

I could. But would I? This was such an unprecedented situation.

'I don't think ...' I began.

'He'll listen to you. I shouldn't be carrying tales, but I couldn't help overhearing him quarrelling with Miss Jenna.'

'What about this time?' I asked resignedly.

'She said something about it being too good an opportunity to miss. He was angry and told her to shut up.'

'I expect he'll unburden himself when he's ready,' I said casually. I now know better than to get mixed up in the Reeds' quarrels. I picked up the drawing of the house and mountain. 'I think I'll take this home and see if Felice remembers drawing it. I wonder why she didn't sign it. Did Roger notice?'

'Yes, he did. And if I were you I'd wait until he comes back before showing it to her.'

Davies's manner was so odd, I was about to question him further when I was called to the telephone. The Reeds' housekeeper was on the line, and I was surprised to hear the agitation in her voice.

'There's been a little accident,' she said. 'Miss Jenna's chair overturned. She's in the hospital for a check-up. I haven't a number for Mr Reed. Will you go to the hospital?'

Anxiously I drove to the cottage hospital. Jenna was lying in bed in the small double room, which in fact had been endowed by her father. The second bed was unoccupied.

She was propped up. 'Who sent for you?'

'Miss Linton. She hasn't a number for Roger. Have you?'

A slow smile transformed her features. 'That's a joke! Has Roger forgotten to tell you where he is?'

I ignored this jibe. 'What does the doctor say?'

'He waffled on about my legs. I told him no more operations.'

'Don't be childish, Jenna. How did the accident happen?'

'I was reaching for something,' she said sulkily.

'I'll go and speak to the doctor or the sister,' I said.

'Come back afterwards, Lindsay.' I heard and understood the panic.

The doctor, a new one, told me his name was McIntyre. His interest was paralysis and he wanted to study Jenna's case. He presumed there would be no objection in keeping her in for a few days. Was I a relative?

I explained the position and went back to Jenna.

'Dr McIntyre is interested in your case. He wants to keep you in for a few days. That's OK, isn't it?'

She didn't answer, and to my horror I saw tears rolling down her cheeks. 'Jen, what is it?'

'I can't stay here. I won't. Get Roger.'

'Where is he?'

48

'Paris. Please send for him.' She reached for her handbag and passed me a folded piece of paper. I took it and stood up, but she clutched at my hand, twining her fingers tightly in mine so I couldn't break loose.

'You don't know how awful it is to be trapped in that chair all the time. I wish I'd been the one to die.'

'Jen, you mustn't say that. You're young and beautiful ...'

'And helpless. Useless too. You've said so a thousand times. No one understands, not even Roger. And he doesn't care.'

'That's not true Jen. Roger cares a great deal about you.'

'Do you?'

The direct question threw me. If I had ever examined my feelings towards Jenna, I came up against an immediate stumbling block: the accident. And before that time I had hardly known her. True, I pitied her, but I hadn't ever put myself in her place, and now I did, I was aware of my lack of sensitivity.

Her eyes were soft, pleading.

I had to be honest. 'The accident has been between us—but now ...'

'I need a friend,' she said urgently. 'You, Lindsay. I don't suppose Felice will ever forgive, but you are different.'

I looked at her lying propped up on the pillows, and was overwhelmed by a feeling of protectiveness. I bent and kissed her cheek.

49

'Ask Roger to come soon,' she whispered.

*   *   *

I telephoned Roger that evening.

'Lindsay. I didn't ...'

'That's right. You didn't tell me where you'd be. Jenna gave me your phone number. She's had a bit of an accident, fell out of her chair and is in the hospital.'

'Oh God,' he groaned. 'Is she badly hurt?'

'No. But she wants you.'

There was a lengthening silence. At last I said, 'Roger?'

'All right. I can't get back tomorrow. I'll try and get a flight for the following day.'

'But ...' I began. But he rang off.

His behaviour was inexplicable. Never in the three years we had worked in close liaison, had he set me aside without explanation. By the time he arrived just before closing-time two days later, my frustration and anger had reached boiling point.

I was in the office entering the sales in the ledger, so he was standing at the door before I realised he was there.

'I've been to the hospital. Jen says you've been very kind. I've persuaded her to stay in while the doctor completes his tests.'

'Good,' I said briskly.

'You're angry.'

'Yes, I am.'

'I didn't mean to upset you. I expected to come back the next day. I can't talk about my business in Paris at the moment.'

I accepted his explanation with as good a grace as possible. After all, as Jenna so often reminded me, I was only an employee. Granted, he may have family business, and I comforted myself that this was probably the answer and had nothing to do with the Gallery. Our mutual trust seemed to have lessened, and yet in some strange way I felt he hated not confiding in me.

Even his gift of an exquisite bottle of scent had the undertones of a bribe, a means of shutting me up. I took the hint, and left him to his own devices.

*   *   *

I was now unashamedly looking forward to my boat trip with Philippe. We needed the kind of day which endows lake and mountains with that special quality that transforms the landscape into an unforgettable memory. We were vouchsafed such a day.

We boarded the hired motorboat at the jetty in Longmere. It was called *Water Sprite* and lived up to its name, fairly dancing to Philippe's masterly control.

I sat back, one arm round Barney. The motion and the rapidly changing scenery gave me a sensation of sheer exuberance.

51

Philippe was keeping a keen look-out for a landing place, and we both saw a shallow inlet, a pebble bright silver of shore, and overhanging trees; a green gloom reflected in the water.

'Perfect,' I said as he beached the boat.

'I didn't know such days were possible.' Philippe lugged the enormous hamper containing food and lord knows what to a convenient spot. 'Even France can't compare with this. Let's celebrate.'

He opened the hamper, and lifted out two glasses and a bottle of champagne. It frothed into the glasses, amber yellow in the sun.

'To us, Lindsay.'

'To us.'

I leant back against a convenient rock, now sun-warmed, and sipped the wine, and tried to see the lake and mountains as if I had Felice's eyes. Why was she able to transmute such ordinary natural objects like a lake and mountains into a heart-catching picture?

As if reading my thoughts, Philippe said, 'How would your mother see this?' He paused, and then continued, 'I suppose the truth is, she has perception to see beyond the obvious. I envy her.'

I suppose I did too. But I'd never admit it.

I told Philippe about the picture I'd discovered tucked away in the stockroom. Roger agreed with me it would be right to show it to Felice, and if she admitted it was her work, include it in the exhibition.

Philippe's interest quickened. 'Is it the same view as mine?'

'Similar. But there is something in it I can't quite put my finger on. It will be interesting to know which she painted first.'

'Will we ever find her dream house?' he asked wistfully.

'If it is only a dream, will it matter to you?'

'Oh yes. I came here to find it.' He moved close to my side. His finger, delicate as a butterfly alighted on my arm, his slight pressure more exciting than a kiss. I shivered and drew away.

'Let's open your hamper.'

He unpacked the sort of food I'd expected, a Fortnum and Mason's spread, and we ate with relish. We finished the bottle of wine, and then stowed the hamper back in the boat. I suggested we shifted the boat and moored it at the private jetty belonging to family friends. Philippe demurred.

'They have a super collection of Felice's pictures.'

He grinned. 'The carrot dangling in front of the donkey's nose.'

'Not quite. The Outhwaites' house is next door to the house which belonged to my father's family. It was sold when Grandmother died. The Outhwaites are very fond of Felice, and will be hurt if I don't give them a special invitation to her exhibition.'

The Outhwaites were gardening. They always were—in all weathers. Theirs was one of the show gardens on this gentle stretch of Sweetwater, blessed with a lake frontage and an unparalleled view.

Philippe tied up the boat, and we jumped ashore. Peggy came bustling down the path to greet us. Dick followed more leisurely.

She clasped me in her arms. 'Darling, how lovely to see you. I was only saying to Dick it's ages since we visited.'

They had grown alike; thin, skin like shiny chestnuts, startling blue eyes. I introduced Philippe.

Peggy's gaze sharpened. 'Have we met before?'

'I don't think so,' he said, shaking hands.

'Odd, I thought—oh well, I'm always making mistakes aren't I, Dick?'

'Too true.' He grasped my hand and I kissed his cheek.

'Come away in—we'll have tea.' Peggy led the way up the steep path.

The informality of the garden was pleasing and absolutely right. Outcrops of rock were burdened with alpine plants, and tiny lawns were enclosed by hedges of old-fashioned briar roses. Seats were dotted about in strategic places. The house was on higher ground; long and low it seemed to be wallowing in a trough of foliage.

We entered the drawing-room from the
54

terrace. The picture windows were open to their fullest extent, and the room gave the impression of being a continuation of the garden.

I accompanied Peggy to the kitchen. 'How is Felice?' she asked.

'Busy. We're having an exhibition of her work in the Gallery in August. Maybe you and Dick will come.'

'Of course. We wouldn't miss it for anything.' She arranged cakes on a plate. 'A new young man?' she said with a wicked grin.

'Come off it, Peggy. He isn't my young man.' I paused. 'He's an admirer of Felice's art.'

'He reminds me of someone ...'

'Probably a telly star.'

She shrugged. 'We don't see enough of you and Felice.'

'I know. The Gallery keeps me busy, and Felice is working hard. She misses my father.'

Peggy sighed and brewed the tea, and I wheeled the trolley into the drawing-room.

It was like old happy times, I thought, handing round cups and offering cake. Times, when the three of us, Felice, Con and I had spent fun evenings with Peggy and Dick, singing folk songs and playing silly card games. Con always cheated.

Peggy was deeply interested in people. Felice thought Peggy allotted her friends little compartments and labelled them with the occupations. Like, Felice is an artist, Lindsay runs an Art Gallery, and now, Philippe?

'Are you on holiday?' she asked him.

'Long vacation. I teach.'

Dick said, 'Oh yes. What are your subjects?'

'French and history.'

'There's a coincidence, isn't it Dick? My husband has written a history of the Lakeland families, and a wee book about the architecture of some of the old houses. Felice did the illustrations.'

'Good lord, I'd forgotten.' I smiled at Philippe. 'Dick's books are in the Gallery bookshop.'

His eyes gleamed. It was as if he had uncovered the first clue on a long treasure hunt, and he was determined to win the prize.

'Lindsay says you are interested in Felice's work. We have a small collection. Would you like to see them?' she asked Philippe.

He stood up immediately, and Peggy said, 'We keep them in the dining-room. It's the only north-facing room in the house.'

She ushered us across the hall and threw open the door. Felice's pictures covered two walls. Their pride in their home ground was reflected in the choice of pictures. Here was the softer, gentler aspects unshadowed by the thrusting peaks which excited so many people.

Felice's treatment of water was masterly. The lakes dominated her pictures, and as always I marvelled at her superb artistry. Philippe studied each picture with care. I

56

guessed he was seeking confirmation that the one in his possession of the house Felice had painted wasn't just a figment of her imagination. Only one of the Outhwaites' pictures gave the impression of a house—a distant view—and again I noted the strange shift in the time sequence.

Philippe turned abruptly to Dick. 'Does this particular house figure in your book?' he asked pointing to it.

Dick peered closely at the picture, and there was a puzzled look in his eyes. Peggy stepped forward.

'No.' She gave no explanation, but she cast a wary look at Dick.

'Is it real?' Philippe asked.

Peggy laughed. 'You've met Felice, haven't you? Who knows what is real to her.' She took hold of his arm and guided him in front of a picture luminous with feeling. A glimpse of water, sky, a clump of conifers, a suggestion of high peaks. 'This is my favourite.'

CHAPTER FIVE

'I think your friends know that house,' Philippe said, when he came into the Gallery the next day to buy Dick Outhwaite's books.

I'd had the same impression, but didn't think it would help matters by saying so.

'Perhaps your mother bought those pictures because she liked them, and they have no special significance,' I suggested.

He shook his head. 'She didn't share them with anyone, not even me, until it was too late. I'm sorry to be such an awful bore, Lindsay. Can you spare the time to have a drink?'

I glanced at my watch. 'Thanks, but I can't. I promised to take some stuff up to Jenna in the hospital.'

'May I come with you? I can wait outside.'

'No need. Jen will be delighted to see you. In fact, she hoped you'd call in at the Gallery when she was there.'

He smiled. 'I'll buy her a few flowers.'

He bought an enormous bunch of roses, carnations and spiky blue delphiniums, and drove us to the hospital. As always it was difficult to park, and Philippe dropped me at the door and suggested I went ahead. Outside Jenna's room I encountered John Ritter.

He stopped and took my arm. 'I want to talk to you,' he said truculently. A scowl marred the smoothness of his high forehead, and his thin mouth was lost in a bushy beard.

'Not here. I'll be pleased to talk to you at the Gallery.'

'You won't be pleased when you hear what I have to say.'

'That will be for me to judge.' I disengaged my arm, and walked past him into Jenna's room.

'What was Ritter doing here?'

Jenna was sitting in a chair by the window. A shaft of sunshine threw up warm colours in her hair, emphasising her ethereal look.

'Why shouldn't he visit? He's a friend.'

'Roger doesn't approve of him, and he's cross about you accepting Ritter's pictures without asking.'

'He doesn't make any fuss about how many of Felice's are unloaded on us. Anyway, who is Roger to judge Ritter?'

'Oh Jen,' I moaned. 'You must know the kind of man Ritter is.'

'What if I do,' she said defiantly.

I put the basket down on the table near her. 'Your shopping.'

She smiled. 'Thanks, Lindsay.'

'What is the doctor's latest report?'

'Great.' Her eyes shone. 'He says I can go home tomorrow for a week or two.'

'But I thought ...'

She interrupted. 'I've agreed to go into a clinic in Hungary.'

'That's good. I'm glad.'

'Are you Lindsay?' Her mouth dropped.

'Come on, Jen, buck up. You've got guts or Con wouldn't have taken you climbing with him.'

She scrubbed her eyes. 'He thought a lot of me.'

'I'm sure he did. He liked kids with guts.'

'Did he take you climbing?' she said.

'Sometimes.' I had never admitted my fear of heights, not even to my father.

There was a tentative knock on the door, and Philippe put his head round the jamb. 'May I come in?'

Jenna's face lit up. Her eyes sparkled, a flush coloured her cheeks. She was so beautiful.

Philippe entered the room, and laid his flowers in her lap.

'How absolutely super of you to come and bring me flowers.' She shot a baleful look at me. 'You didn't tell me you knew him.'

Philippe smiled. 'But we know each other too.'

'I don't know your name.'

'Philippe Deauville.'

An odd look crossed her face. 'Philippe Deauville,' she repeated. 'I thought of lots of names, but not Philippe.' Her eyes clouded. 'You are mean Lindsay. I suppose you want to keep him for yourself.'

'Hey, wait a minute!' Philippe perched on the bed. 'I introduced myself to Lindsay's mother. I'm interested in her work.'

'Oh Felice,' she said, 'always Felice. Con talked about her all the time we were climbing that last time. Felice, Felice. I was mad, and . . .' She stopped speaking.

For the first time I experienced at second hand something of the tension that must have existed between this girl and my father. Had Con being trying to tell Jenna something?

Warning the seventeen-year-old girl Felice was his life?

'Felice is a great artist,' Philippe said. 'I admire her work.'

'And her, no doubt. Everyone thinks Felice is wonderful—but I know—lots of things.'

'More of your lies, Jenna. I warn you I won't hear a word against my mother. Is that clear?'

Philippe's glance met mine. He raised his brows interrogatively. I shook my head. I hadn't realised how much Jenna hated Felice.

'Does Roger know you are coming home tomorrow?'

She nodded. 'He knows, but he's sending Linton in a taxi.' She looked at Philippe, lips pouting. 'Roger's sick of his little sister. I stand in the way of his marriage plans. Don't I, Lindsay?'

'For heaven's sake, Jenna. You know that's not true.'

'You would say that,' she retorted. 'In your eyes Roger can do no wrong.'

'Perhaps I can be of some assistance?' Philippe said. 'May I have the pleasure of taking you home?'

His slightly formal manner jarred, but not on Jenna.

'Would you? Would you really? That would be absolutely super.' They arranged the time and details.

I listened with growing tension; wishing I hadn't put so much credence on my outings

61

with Philippe. I began to feel that his only interest in me was because he admired Felice's work and my usefulness in tracking down the location of his wretched pictures.

I stood up. 'I have to go.'

Philippe rose too.

'Must you go so soon, Philippe?' Jenna's look pleaded.

'Do stay,' I said coldly. 'I can walk back.'

'Don't be silly, Lindsay.' His tone was sharp. He smiled at Jenna. 'Until tomorrow.'

He didn't speak until he parked outside the Gallery. 'Have dinner with me tonight, Lindsay, please?'

'Thanks, but I can't,' I said, without explanation.

*   *   *

Felice was in the studio when I arrived home. She was standing in the middle of the floor, her expression sad, her mouth drooped.

'What's the matter, Felice?'

She glared at me. 'I wish that Frenchman had never come. It doesn't do to disturb the past. Better to let the layers of time cover it.'

'What are you talking about?' I said irritably. 'Surely Philippe has a right to try and trace the house which he believes has connections with his mother. I think both you and the Outhwaites know where it is. Is it haunted or something?'

62

'Haunted?' She started. 'There is no such house.'

I always know when my mother is lying. She turns away her head, and wrings her hands together.

'Why does it haunt you?'

'Haunt me!' she exclaimed. 'Not me—others perhaps. Yes, others, the end of an era which none of them wanted to end.'

'Who are they? And it is a real place,' I accused.

'People. People I've forgotten.'

'I don't believe you. You are making a mystery out of something quite ordinary, and misleading Philippe. I'm sick of the whole thing.'

'Good. Then you can forget it.' She seemed to emerge from a disquieting despondency, displaying the same kind of transformation as does a caterpillar blossoming into a butterfly. Colour sprang into her cheeks and she lost her intense expression, straightening her body and becoming charged with energy.

'Come on, Lindsay, we're late. We are eating dinner at Dora's.'

My own depression lifted. Dora made a party of a simple dinner, and she was a superb cook. I determined to put all my niggling worries out of my mind, and enjoy a leisurely dinner.

By the time we reached the coffee and liqueurs stage, my mind was pleasantly empty

63

of all except the enjoyment of good food.

Dora was not a great drinker. After two glasses of wine she lapsed into sentimental reminiscences.

'That boy, Philippe, he reminds me of someone. Can't just think who it is. But it's there sitting at the back of my mind.'

'Don't be ridiculous, Dora,' Felice said.

Dora shook her head. 'It's that little trick he has of widening his eyes. Like someone we once knew. Felice, can't you think?'

'He reminded the Outhwaites of someone too,' I said.

Felice dismissed the idea as tosh. I wasn't convinced, and neither was Dora. Once an idea lodged in her mind she scrabbles away at it. It seemed to me at this moment, a little hazy with wine, that I too was teetering on the edge of some chasm, which, if I fell in would change the whole course of my life. Mentally I shook myself; having fancies as Felice did wouldn't do.

Con had shown the way; taut with professionalism, relying on facts and precise information, taking clear decisions. That had been the secret of his success as a climber, and it had ended because of a girl's unpredictability. Or had her young beauty pierced the skin of his resolve?

'I'll think who it is,' Dora said, 'or I'll get no rest.'

Felice was angry. Her eyes glinted, and her

hands clenched. 'I don't want to hear another word about that Frenchman.'

'Half French, Felice. His mother was English,' I said.

Dora pouted. 'I like him. Lovely manners. He took me out to tea.'

Felice said, 'You never told me.'

Dora shrugged. 'You didn't want to know.'

Their friendship was founded on their outspokenness.

'I don't see any harm in him wanting to find out his mother's background. I've promised to help him,' Dora said defiantly.

Felice glared at her. 'How?'

Dora smiled. 'I'll think of a way. It's tough not knowing who your maternal grandparents are, or your family history.' She paused to see what effect her words were having on us. 'I'm tracing my family history,' she continued. 'I've had no trouble looking up the Crumbs. Born and died in this area for the last three hundred years. How about the Flytes?' She looked hard at Felice.

The Flytes were a sore point with Felice. She had abandoned or been abandoned by her father long ago. Her mother was dead. Her father had married for a second time. Felice said her step-mother was a tart he'd picked up in a pub.

I stood up. 'Bed. I've an early start tomorrow.'

'You work too hard,' Dora was

sympathetic. 'That Roger Reed has no thought for you.'

'Not right, Dora. Roger is very considerate. We make a good team.'

Next morning my team-mate was in the Gallery before me. He was sitting at the desk opening the mail. He looked tired and vulnerable.

'You look spent,' I said, taking the chair opposite him.

'Was it your idiot idea to encourage Deauville to take Jen home from the hospital? You know how easily impressed she is. Before we know where we are she's going to imagine herself wildly in love with him.'

'Well, it might put that awful Ritter out of her mind.'

'Ritter!'

'He was visiting her in the hospital.'

'What! I've forbidden her ...'

'She's stubborn, Roger. She'll defy you on principle.'

'Did you speak to him?'

I nodded. 'He was very aggressive. I told him if he'd anything to say, to come here.'

'Are his pictures still around?'

'Yes. There are a couple of charcoal drawings I thought ...'

'No. No.' Roger banged the desk. 'If he turns up while I'm away, tell him to remove the lot. And keep Davies in the office while you are talking to him. I don't trust him.'

'We're making an enemy,' I said quietly.

'We have already.'

Roger pushed the mail across the desk. 'There's a letter from the Wilder Gallery about taking Felice's exhibition on to them when it closes here. That should please her.'

We continued to discuss the details of the exhibition which was due to open in a week's time. There had been a good response from the press, and we anxiously reviewed the list of invited guests. Felice's work was almost a cult on her home ground, and the local fan club wanted a special showing. We agreed a date, and Roger relaxed when he realised all the arrangements were in hand.

We were just about to go and have a snack lunch when Jenna phoned. I could hear the jubilation in her voice. Philippe had driven her home, and we weren't to worry about her. He'd promised to stay to lunch and keep her company until Roger returned.

Suddenly I was jealous and uneasy. Jenna would stir up trouble if she could. Would Philippe believe her? Why not?

'I want to talk to Felice,' Roger said later in the afternoon.

'OK. Come home with me. We can rustle up a meal.'

'Make it tomorrow. I'd better get home and see what my little sister is doing.' He grinned. 'She isn't to be trusted.'

Dora was waiting for me at the gate. She beckoned urgently and I parked the car and followed her into her cottage.

'When I had tea with Philippe,' she said, 'he showed me his pictures. And I've been thinking about them. Soon after Felice and Con were married, they had a big row. We couldn't help hearing them,' she said virtuously. 'Felice cleared off, and she was away a week, and when she came back she showed me a picture. It was of a house, exactly like the one in Philippe's pictures. I asked where it was, and she just smiled, and said it was a secret. I surmised she didn't want Con to know where she'd been.'

'So there really is a house,' I mused.

'She caught a bus,' Dora said, 'because my Bert spoke to her at the stop. She said she was going to stay with friends. It was the Grasmere bus,' she added triumphantly. 'Shall I tell Philippe?'

'Sure. You'll find him at the Reeds' house.'

'What's he doing there?'

'Keeping Jenna company.'

She looked at me strangely. 'I hope you know what you are doing,' she said.

CHAPTER SIX

Ritter called at the Gallery while Roger was out.

Davies announced him. I felt a moment's panic. 'OK, show him in but stay here in the office. Roger's orders,' I added.

'Where's Reed?' Ritter demanded, marching into the office.

'He's busy.'

'He would be. Leaves all his dirty work to his little yes-woman.'

I felt my colour rising. 'Wouldn't it be a good idea if you just take your canvases as Mr Reed requested in his letter?'

'That would suit you.' He sat down heavily. His face was flushed, and I could smell the whisky on his breath across the desk.

'Mr Ritter,' I said slowly and clearly, 'your canvases were brought here without Mr Reed's knowledge or agreement. He is under no obligation to accept or show them. So please take them away.'

'So Jenna is right. She doesn't count in this set-up.' His eyes were red-rimmed, and he squinted across at me as if he was having difficulty in focusing. 'She told me I'd have to sweeten you first.'

'You are being objectionable.'

Davies moved to the back of my chair. How

grateful I was for his strength and stability, his complete loyalty.

Ritter glared at him. 'My paintings are just as good as Flyte's,' he whined. 'Everyone says so.'

'Then you'll have no trouble placing them elsewhere.'

He leant forward, elbows on the desk, and buried his face in his hands. His behaviour was beginning to frighten me, and I wished Roger was here with his added authority. I picked up the house telephone and ordered black coffee.

Ritter was watching me through his outspread fingers. When the coffee arrived, he put down his hands and stirred in sugar.

'It is quite impossible for me to take away my canvases.' His voice was dangerously quiet. 'I thought Jenna explained. She knows they have to stay here until ...' He paused to drink his coffee.

'That's not possible,' I said. 'We want the space.'

'For some more of Miss Flyte's pictures, I suppose,' he sneered. 'I have no intention of removing them until both Jenna and Reed say so. And certainly not on your instructions.'

He stood up, supporting himself for a moment against the edge of the desk. 'Goodbye, Miss Strong.' He staggered to the door. Davies opened it and followed him out into the Gallery.

I was angry and humiliated. Had Jenna

70

encouraged him to put me in my place which was obviously Ritter's object, or had he some other reason for not removing the pictures?

Davies came back. 'I've seen him off the premises, Miss Lindsay. Take no notice of his rudeness. Did Miss Jenna make a note in the book of the number of pictures he left here?'

'I hope so,' I said, turning back the pages. 'When was it?'

Davies thought. 'It was the day you and Mr Reed were at the auction in London. I tried to stop her accepting them. She told me to mind my own business, and he carried them into the stockroom. Both of them were in there some time.'

'She didn't enter them into the book.'

'I thought not. When they had gone I went and looked through them. There were ten canvases. I'm sure of that. I made a note in my diary.' He produced the book and showed me the entry. 'I've a feeling he may try and pull a fast one on us.'

Davies filled the electric kettle, switched on, and made tea.

'I don't like this.' I sipped my tea gratefully.

'No more do I. It's up to Mr Reed to sort it out. Don't you worry, Miss Lindsay, it's not your problem.'

I wasn't too sure about that. But Davies was the great comforter. I felt nothing could be really bad while he looked at the question with such a matter of fact approach.

71

I longed for Roger's return, but the day wore on, and he didn't come. In desperation I phoned his home number.

Jenna answered. 'Oh it's you. Roger isn't here. You should keep track of him better. You're slipping, dear Miss Strong.' She laughed and put down the receiver.

Damn the Reeds, I thought, as Davies and I locked up. Outside the sun silvered the lake, and Philippe wasn't waiting for me.

*   *   *

Philippe came into the Gallery the next day about lunch-time.

'What's the matter, Lindsay?'

I hadn't realised I must look as distraught as I felt, but I certainly couldn't discuss Roger's peculiar behaviour with Philippe. Roger had disappeared. That sounded dramatic, but it was the cold truth. There had been no word from him either to me or Jenna. She had telephoned late last night. She was obviously upset at Roger's non-return. I was just furious.

Jenna phoned again early in the morning. Her voice sounded tearful. 'He didn't come back last night. I waited up until two o'clock. It's my fault, Lindsay. We had a row. I was awful to him.'

My heart sank. 'What about?' I asked coldly.

'Nothing to do with you. Family. And you

72

aren't family—yet.'

I was certain I never would be family, but I was sad nothing had really changed between us. In the hospital she had needed me, a friend. Now she did not. I knew in my heart our differences were too deep to be overcome easily.

The morning was not going smoothly. Already I'd had to deal with several customers who demanded to speak to Roger, and the final straw came when Davies announced there was a bloke to see Roger.

'Who?'

'Detective Sergeant Brack. He says he has an appointment with Mr Reed. Will you see him?'

I nodded. At least it couldn't be bad news about Roger if he was expecting to talk to him.

The Sergeant was big, bluff and had hard unyielding eyes. I guessed he wouldn't show much mercy to villains.

'There's a gang of picture thieves around.' He sat down and accepted the offer of a cup of coffee. 'I thought I'd better warn you and check up on your security arrangements.'

I explained about the working of the burglar alarm, the locks on doors and windows, and the combination lock on the small strong-room door where we kept a few valuable paintings, mostly ones Roger was commissioned to buy.

'That all sounds satisfactory, perhaps I'd better take a look.'

He went off with Davies, and I sat back with a sigh of relief. The mail lay unopened on the desk, and I sorted it out. It was only a few days to the opening and although plans were well in hand, I felt there were details Roger should make a decision on, and put in hand. So where was he?

The desk diary revealed nothing except scribbled initials. No time or place, and no help at all. So it was not surprising I was pleased to see Philippe.

'What you need my dear Lindsay is food and drink.'

'I can't leave the office,' I said.

'Why not?'

'I'm waiting for a phone call.'

Davies stepped forward. 'I can take any calls, Miss Lindsay.'

Reluctantly I left with Philippe, consoling myself with the thought that if Roger phoned I might well lose my temper. The bar in the Harriers Arms was busy. However Philippe secured a small table, and went up to the bar to order food and fetch our drinks. Returning, he put the glasses on the table, and smiled. Unaccountably my spirits revived. Philippe's warm smile renewed confidence.

'What's your problem?' he said.

If I could have spoken the truth I would have said, the Reeds. Instead I said, 'Just the usual hassle.'

'I don't believe you, Lindsay. You are the

soul of efficiency, the envy of young Jenna, and very, very attractive when you wrinkle your brow.'

'Oh shut up, Philippe,' I laughed.

'That's better.' He grinned, and reaching for my hand, squeezed it.

'Has Roger turned up?' he asked abruptly. 'Jenna phoned me at the crack of dawn. They had a right royal row—unfortunately part of it in my hearing. He's got a problem with that girl.'

'What were they quarrelling about?'

He hesitated. 'Some artist fellow.'

'Ritter,' I breathed the name. 'Jenna is so gullible.'

'I wouldn't say that. She's a calculating little madam, and I don't like her attitude to you and Felice.'

Somehow I thought he was being too vehement. Jenna's enchanting face materialised in my mind's eye. Had she already hooked Philippe? To take my thoughts off Jenna I asked him if Dora Crumb had imparted her information about Felice's activities so many years ago.

'Do you think there is anything in it?' he asked.

'I don't know. If it was a real house, surely someone would have recognised it. Are you sure your mother came from this district?'

'I'm not sure about anything,' he sighed. 'Lindsay, may I come to the opening of the

75

exhibition?'

'I should be upset if you didn't.'

He smiled. 'Do you think it would be a good idea if I brought my pictures? Not for sale,' he added hastily. 'But someone might give us a lead as to the whereabouts of that house if it is real.'

I hesitated. 'As far as I'm concerned that will be OK, but I'll have to sound out Roger.'

Sounding out Roger wasn't going to be easy. He didn't communicate the next day and I had a hysterical girl on my hands.

I appealed to Philippe. 'You're used to kids. What do I do?'

'Jenna is hardly a kid, but I get your meaning. The boys in my class suffer from the same sense of insecurity, at least some of them do. Broken homes play havoc with the youngsters. I think we must reassure her.'

'How? I haven't an idea where Roger is, or if he's met with an accident. Do you think I ought to go to the police?'

'They won't be interested unless you can be more specific.'

Philippe arranged to pick up Jenna, and take her to the Lake End Hotel for dinner, where I was to meet them. Miss Linton would man the phone, and opined it would do Jenna good to get out of the house. She was probably feeling the strain of Jenna's hysterics.

I joined them in the cocktail lounge. Hesitating in the doorway I looked across the room. Jenna wore a long flame-coloured dress. Her hair was held back by a red velvet ribbon, and curls framed her face. She was looking up at Philippe, and my heart missed a beat as I saw him touch her cheek. If I could have decently turned away, I would have done so, but at that moment Philippe looked up and waved.

Roger was the phantom at our feast. Through Jenna we glimpsed a different view; assessment of a sister who had lived with him all her life, and was totally aware of his moods.

I was glad when the evening ended. Philippe drove Jenna home, and I returned alone with brooding thoughts. I parked my car, and noticed there was a light on in the sitting-room. I wondered why Felice wasn't in bed, and I hurried in fearing she was unwell.

Roger sat on the sofa with Barney beside him. The dog's head was laid across his knees. All the pent up emotions of the last few days rose to the surface of my mind. I didn't speak, and for an interminable moment or two neither did he. We looked at each other, and at last he said, 'I'm sorry. Were you worried?'

'Yes.'

He nodded. 'I had my reasons.'

'Was Jenna to blame? She's very upset and worried; she thinks it was her fault you stayed away without a word.'

'Partly. She's so wilful; impossible really. In the heat of the moment I walked out. When I cooled down I realised that because she's

77

trapped in a wheelchair I'm treating her like a child.'

'You could be right,' I sighed and took off my coat. 'I'll make coffee.'

Roger followed me into the kitchen.

'Where have you been? Or shouldn't I ask?'

I glanced at him. He was indeed troubled, and immediately my sympathy was roused. I filled the percolator and measured out the coffee.

'Have you eaten, Roger?'

'Eaten? Oh yes, I had a meal on the plane.'

I reached for a tray and the cake tin.

'I meant to phone you, Lindsay. And then I thought she'll worry if I don't. She cares. Silly of me, I suppose.'

'Very silly. Any good assistant worries when her boss clears off without a word, and leaves her holding the baby so to speak.'

'Boss? Do you think of me as your boss?'

'Jenna makes it plain that you and she are Reeds and owners of the Gallery. She also informed me I had no right to enquire into your private affairs.'

'She's jealous—of you.'

'That's stupid.'

'Not really. She knows exactly how deeply I care for you.'

I let that pass, and concentrated on making the coffee. The aroma filled the kitchen. There was an air of domesticity between us which I didn't wish to encourage, and yet Roger looked so at ease sitting at the table, as if he belonged.

'It seems that I'm not only a personal assistant or whatever you like to call me, but some sort of detective as well. I deduce you've been abroad.'

'Oh that—yes.' He didn't offer an explanation.

'Did the quarrel with Jenna drive you away?'

'Quarrel? Who told you?'

'She did. And so did Philippe. He heard part of it.'

A blank expression crossed Roger's face, and he stiffened.

'Let's drink coffee here. I like your orderly kitchen, everything in place and a place for everything. It speaks to me of you, my darling Lindsay. You are so practical.'

I filled the coffee mugs and cut a slice of cake for him.

'Sit down, please Lindsay. I need to talk to you.'

Some of the resentment was disappearing. I had been angry about his secret trip, as I liked to think of it. But where he'd been and why was his business. I pulled out a stool and sat down.

'I suppose Jenna told you I'd issued an ultimatum?' he said.

I shook my head, and dribbled cream into my coffee.

'I can't take much more of her dramatics. She is becoming so intense and wilful. A row

79

blew up between us over John Ritter.'

'I'm not surprised. He is a very dangerous and vindictive man. I had a most unpleasant interview with him. Davies stayed in the office with me, and I was glad of his protection; the bloke was drunk. In any case, he's out to make trouble. Davies agrees with me.'

'Did he take his canvases?'

'No. He refused. He said I was your yes-woman, and he'd only take them away if you or Jenna ordered him. I had the impression he'd made some sort of deal with Jenna; or has he a hold over her?'

'It's possible,' Roger said soberly.

'I don't get it, Roger. Can he be blackmailing her?'

'God knows! She won't talk. But there is something between them.' He helped himself to more coffee. 'It seems I can't trust anyone.'

'What do you mean? Are you implying you can't trust me? If that's the case, I quit.'

He jumped up, and coming round the table pulled me into his arms. 'This Deauville fellow—what have you told him about the Gallery?'

I tried to wriggle out of his arms but he held me fast.

'Look at me, Lindsay.'

I raised my head and our glances met. 'I don't understand. Philippe is a friend. Why should he have more than a passing interest in the Gallery?'

'My guess is he has questioned both you and Jenna, and he's been busy sending reports to the Deauville brothers in Paris.'

'That's the craziest idea I've ever heard. Why should he ...'

I stopped, remembering Philippe's close questioning. My heart leapt with ridiculous guilt. What had I said?

'Don't look so stricken, Lindsay. Fortunately no great harm has been done.' He released me abruptly, and returned to his stool. 'The truth is,' he said, 'the Deauville brothers have made me a very good offer for the Gallery and contents. I'll admit to you I was tempted ...'

'But you can't even think of it,' I interrupted. 'Your father ...'

'That's right. My father would never have forgiven me. But this offer brought me up sharply. I examined my reasons for continuing to run the Gallery.'

'And what are they?'

'Confused. I don't have your logical mind. I only know that my roots are here and if I sold the Gallery I would be nothing.'

'That's not true.'

'Yes, it is, Lindsay. The Gallery is a way of life, my way. I have the same objectives which motivated my father. While we have not produced any artist of note, there has always been this deep respect and belief in the artists who have lived and worked here.'

81

He shifted restlessly on his stool. I was moved by his sincerity, and although I'd always known how deeply he felt about the Gallery I hadn't suspected it meant so much to him.

'You won't be selling?' I said tentatively.

'That's right, Lindsay. I won't be selling.'

I sighed with a relief that didn't lessen the feeling that Philippe had betrayed me.

'And you, my dearest Lindsay, how do you feel about the Gallery? And about me?'

'You know I enjoy working in the Gallery. I love this place too.'

'So you've no thought of "quitting" as you put it?'

'Of course not, Roger.' I paused and looked at him warily.

'I would find it difficult to manage without you—and Davies,' he added. 'But I had a more permanent arrangement in mind—for us.'

My heart began to thump. My mind might be orderly, but my emotions were not.

'I don't think this is the time to talk about permanent arrangements,' I said hastily. 'There is still Jenna to consider. Incidentally, have you let her know you are back? Shouldn't you put her mind at rest?'

'I phoned earlier. Miss Linton said she was dining with Deauville. And you.'

'The unwanted third,' I said flatly.

'That isn't my impression, Lindsay.'

'Well, that's how it is,' I said, more sharply

than I'd intended. 'I hope you aren't going away again. Felice's show opens on Monday.' I paused, 'And there is Ritter.'

I stood up, and he too rose, and adroitly caught me against him. I stiffened, and turned my face away, but it was of no avail. He forced wild kisses on my lips, until he realised he couldn't awaken any response, and pushed me aside.

'If that bloke Deauville has come between us ...' he muttered.

'Don't be foolish, Roger. Hadn't you better go?'

With a muttered goodnight, he walked out of the room and out of the house. I locked up, and rinsed the coffee cups. When I returned to the sitting-room, Felice was draped languidly on the sofa, and Barney had climbed up beside her.

'Why did you let Roger in?' I flung myself into a chair, suddenly bone weary.

Felice closed her eyes, and her hands plucked at the material of her négligé. She was going to skirt round the question, I knew the signs. She only answered when she'd thought out what suited her.

'He brought me a present. Wasn't it sweet of him? He's very nice, really, Lindsay. I hope you aren't making him unhappy.'

'Nothing is further from my thoughts. What's your present?'

She passed me a leather case, and when I

opened it, lying on ivory velvet was an exquisite miniature.

'Roger thought the unknown lady had a look of me. Do you think so, Lindsay?' she asked anxiously.

The painted face bore not the slightest resemblance to Felice. It was the face of youth and innocence and trust, and Felice was none of those things. And yet, I thought, perhaps that was how Felice looked when she was young.

'He could be right. Why is he giving you presents?'

'A token of his regard,' she laughed. 'He mentioned marriage—to you. I told him he'd better get Deauville out of the way.' She paused, and added maliciously, 'Unless Jenna has got her claws in him.'

'Why are you afraid of Philippe? Did you know his mother?'

She opened her eyes wide. 'I've never been to France. He's wasting his time. He'll get no help from me.'

'You've confirmed my belief she did live somewhere near. Well, I've promised Philippe I'll help him, and so I will.'

'Leave it alone, Lindsay. Or you'll be sorry.'

'Why? What are you hiding?'

'Stupid girl,' she said crossly. 'If Deauville's mother had wanted him to know she'd have told him. But she didn't. The past is dead—like my Con.' Tears formed in her eyes and rolled down her cheeks. I pushed Barney off the sofa and sitting beside her took her in my arms.

CHAPTER SEVEN

Saturday morning. A cloud-ridden day, transmuting the light to a uniform grey. Satisfying, because the Gallery would be crowded for the opening of the exhibition of Felice's pictures.

I arrived at the Gallery early, but not before Davies. He answered my ring at the door and let me in.

'Is She well?' he asked.

'I hope so. She was still asleep when I left, but Mrs Crumb will get her here in time.'

He smiled, and together we walked round the Gallery. Davies paused before Philippe's pictures, which Roger had agreed to hang, grumbling because they were taking up selling space.

'Ring a bell, Davies?' I asked.

He frowned. 'Are they early ones? High Sail—odd.'

Davies turned on one of the spotlights, and focused the beam directly first on one picture and then the other. 'Reminds me of the old Percy place, but ...'

'The Percy place?' I repeated. 'Where's that?'

85

'Can't be. Nowhere near High Sail. Must be imagination. Hers or mine.'

'I need to know,' I said quietly.

'That Frenchman is asking around.'

'He isn't a Frenchman. At least his mother was English.'

'He'd best leave it alone.'

'Oh Davies! Stop being exasperating. Leave what alone?'

He turned away, and there was a stubborn unyielding look on his face. The look he wore when Felice was being criticised.

So it came back to Felice.

I went into the office to phone the caterers and the wine merchants. Exhibitions had been old Mr Reed's trump card. He wanted to be accepted as a serious art critic, not just a purveyor of goods. He had taken up Felice early in her career, and I sometimes thought his admiration wasn't just for her art, but went deeper.

Felice arrived on time, accompanied by a flushed and excited Dora. Felice looked astonishingly young in a plain oatmeal-coloured linen dress, and a scarlet chiffon scarf round her neck. She was cool, remote, but underneath her calm exterior I detected the signs of tension. As always she was afraid of the critics.

She greeted Roger and Davies easily, smiling a lot. Jenna had been persuaded to stay away until Felice took her leave. There were a number of collectors and dealers mingling with the invited guests, and I guessed both the Gallery and Felice would have a bonanza. Felice never showed a lot of interest in the sale of her work, and in a strange way dreaded it going to strangers.

Philippe's arrival went unnoticed, until I had a moment to draw breath. I found him talking to Dora. His gaze, however, was trained on the people studying his pictures.

The Outhwaites claimed Felice, flanking her closely; almost like guards, I thought, and wondered why. By lunch-time the invited guests departed, and others were beginning to leave. A number of the pictures bore red sale tickets. Roger was well satisfied.

Felice and Dora went off with the Outhwaites, and Philippe waited for me. Outside the sun was shining. White clouds flitted fitfully across the expanse of blue sky, at the behest of the wind.

'Lunch?' he queried.

I hesitated. I'd had time to think over his betrayal of my confidence, and I was both hurt and angry. I well knew that all's fair in business, and that information is often gained by illegitimate means. But I denied in my heart that Philippe had cold-bloodedly sought my company, and Jenna's too, for the purpose of obtaining details of the Gallery to pass to his brothers.

'Why the hesitation? Another date?'

I shook my head. 'I haven't time,' I prevaricated.

'We can make it quick. I've fixed a lunch box. Don't make me eat alone.'

He touched my bare arm delicately with his open hand, and my nerves responded.

'We could find a quiet place by the lake.'

I agreed reluctantly. My head was spinning, and I felt an extraordinary inertia. Reaction of course. I'd been hyped up for the last few days.

Tourists do not bother with the little inlets, they stick to the town, and the recognised beauty spots. We drove a short way out of Longmere, and parking in a lay-by walked the short distance down to the lake.

Philippe carried the basket, and as soon as we were settled, unpacked it, and spread the food out on a cloth.

'Courtesy of the Lake End Hotel. They have the right ideas of what to pack in picnic baskets,' he said, uncorking a bottle of wine.

It was odd, but this was the first time since I'd met him that I felt out of tune with him. His perception was acute, and in a little while he asked me what was troubling me.

'I think you know,' I said quietly.

'If you are upset about Jenna ...?'

'No,' I interrupted him. 'Why did you use me and Jenna to gain information about the Gallery? Was that the reason you forced yourself on Felice and me? Well, Roger has turned down you and your brothers.'

A pained look crossed his face.

'And another thing,' I was now in full spate, 'I don't believe all that stuff about wanting to trace the house in your pictures. You wanted to buy us out of the Gallery.'

I emptied my glass, and silently he refilled it.

'Well!' I flashed at him. 'Haven't you got anything to say?'

'Plenty. Calm down, Lindsay. I'm kicking myself for not telling you about my brothers' interest in the Gallery before you found out from Roger. Anything you or Jenna said may have whetted my interest, but my brothers are businessmen and they went through the proper channels.'

'You mean you weren't spying?'

'Do I look like a spy?' he laughed. 'Come on, Lindsay.'

'But Roger said you'd sent your brothers information.'

'I gave them my impression of a lovingly kept Gallery. A place where the Lakeland artists could be sure of a showing. My brothers' business has nothing to do with me.'

'Are you saying that discovering about your mother's pictures was the real reason for seeking out Felice?'

'Of course.' He sounded irritable. 'Are you satisfied I haven't betrayed your confidence?'

I nodded. 'Philippe—I feel awful.'

'Don't.' He bent forward and kissed me on both cheeks. 'Friends?'

'Friends,' I repeated, stifling the longings which almost overwhelmed me. I wanted so much more than friendship from Philippe Deauville.

'Good. I value your friendship, Lindsay.' He smiled, and happiness warmed my heart.

A few minutes later he suggested we walked to Tarn Hows when I had a free day.

'Tarn Hows?' I repeated. 'What put that idea into your head?' And unexpectedly I remember a conversation between Felice and Coniston which had taken place years ago. Perhaps it was still clear in my mind because it had degenerated into a quarrel, and was the only time I'd ever heard them have a disagreement. I couldn't, of course recall the exact words, but Tarn Hows figured contentiously, and Felice's anguished cry was a vivid memory. Why had she cried out so despairingly—'How can I forget. She won.'? It struck me now as it had done then to be totally out of context. I had never questioned them, and until now I hadn't thought it of any significance.

'Dora suggested I should see it before I leave.'

'Leave? But you can't.'

'Dora thinks I should. She says I'm making Felice unhappy, and I don't want to do that. But it is important to me to go on searching for that house.'

'I think you're wasting your time,' I said stiffly. 'If the house was important to your

90

mother surely she would have mentioned it.'

'She didn't. She never mentioned her life in England.'

'Perhaps you have no right to dig into her past life. Maybe there was something she wished to conceal.'

'There was,' he said grimly. 'The name of my father.'

'Philippe, I don't understand.'

'Simple, my dear Lindsay. When André Deauville died, I presumed as his eldest son I would inherit the château and estate. It had never been mentioned certainly, and my mother had insisted I took up a teaching career in England. But you see, Lindsay, I am not a Deauville at all, although I bear my step-father's name. His Will made it clear that I was born before he had even met my mother.'

'Oh Philippe, what an awful shock. I am sorry.' I put my hand on his arm, but he gently disengaged it.

'I'm not looking for pity. And don't think I blame my step-father. It is right a true Deauville should inherit the estate. But you see, Lindsay, I must know who I really am. I must know whose blood runs in my veins. Do you understand my obsession?'

'Yes, I do. I can see it matters a lot to you. But will anyone else care?'

'The woman I may marry. The children, perhaps.'

'The woman who loves you won't care,' I

said softly.

'Wrong. My fiancée broke off our engagement when she discovered I wasn't the Deauville heir.'

'Then she didn't love you.'

He laughed. 'You are right. She has transferred her affections to my step-brother.' He stood up and walked the few steps to the water's edge. I could not gauge the depth of his hurt, and I couldn't think of any way to comfort him.

I got to my feet and began to pack away the remains of the picnic into the basket. He turned to face me, but the sun was behind him, and I couldn't see the expression on his face.

'I'm sorry, Lindsay. I've no right to bother you with my problems. But I hoped Felice ...'

'If you still want my help, it's yours.'

'I do,' he said passionately, and putting his arms round me kissed me on each cheek. How could I now expect more?

'Don't let them force me to leave, not yet.'

'I promise.'

His hands tightened on my arms, and this time he kissed me gently on the mouth, as if to seal a bargain.

* * *

Roger was in the office when I arrived back at the Gallery. He looked pointedly at his wristwatch, which reminded me forcibly I was only an employee.

'Dora has been on the phone. Felice is ill,' he said.

'Ill? She was perfectly all right ...'

'You'd better go home. It's damned awkward when we're busy.'

'I'm sorry Roger, but I must go to her.'

He nodded, and then relented with a wintry smile. 'We'll manage.'

Dora was on the doorstep. 'I'm sorry Lindsay. But Felice insisted I send for you. Roger was quite angry.'

'What's the matter?' I took off my jacket in the hall.

'She won't say. I've got her to bed, but I thought I'd better not send for the doctor until you came.'

Felice was lying flat in the bed in the darkened room. I paused in the doorway, aware of her dependence on me, unrelenting since Con's death. She opened her eyes as I sat down.

'Why have you been so long? Con would have been here immediately.'

'I'm not Con, and I've come as soon as I could.'

'You always put me last,' she whined.

'Don't be silly Felice. Where's your pain?'

'All over,' she moaned. 'Have you phoned the doctor?'

I went downstairs and phoned Dr Marchant. He and my father had been friends, and they had both indulged Felice without thought of the burden now placed on me.

Fortunately Dr Marchant only lived a short distance away, and he arrived in a few minutes. 'Sudden, isn't it? She was perfectly all right when I spoke to her at the exhibition this morning.' He plodded up the stairs and into Felice's bedroom.

Dora was in the kitchen making tea.

'What happened?' I asked. 'I thought you were lunching with the Outhwaites.'

'We did. At the Lake End Hotel. Then Felice said she had a headache and they brought us home. When we got in the house, she kind of collapsed. You don't think it's serious, Lindsay?' Her round ruddy face was full of concern. She put the teapot on the tray and carried it into the sitting-room. 'I'll go,' she said nervously. 'Will you fetch me as soon as Dr Marchant goes?'

In a few minutes he came downstairs and dropped into a chair. I put a cup of tea beside him, and he smiled gratefully.

'Don't worry, Lindsay. Rest and quiet and she'll be fine in a day or two. Tension, excitement, she's highly strung.' He picked up his cup and drank thirstily. I refilled it. 'She's got something on her mind. Coniston knew how to make her talk it out. But I guess now he isn't here she bottles it up. Any idea what it is?'

I shook my head.

'Oh well, I've given her a sedative; she'll

probably sleep for a few hours. Try talking to her, Lindsay.'

I showed the doctor out, and went upstairs. Felice was sleeping, her hand beneath her cheek, her body curled up and relaxed. Dora popped back, and offered to sit with her until she woke.

I drove back to the Gallery. Roger was talking to a customer, and Jenna was ensconced in the office.

'We didn't expect you back. Felice is a leech. Why don't you bust free?'

'She is dependent on me; the same way you are dependent on Roger.'

She flushed. 'It's not the same thing. She only wants masses of attention.'

'So do you, Jenna.'

'Philippe thinks you treat me badly.'

'That's his privilege.'

'I told him you couldn't forgive me because you think I caused Coniston's death. Philippe is taking me out to dinner tonight.'

'Good. Now shut up, and let me get some work done.'

She wheeled herself out of the office, and down the Gallery. Davies knocked on the door and came in. 'Is She all right?'

'The doctor says she's suffering from tension, and over-excitement. She's sleeping. Dora is with her.'

'That's good news. I thought ...' He paused and shut the office door, and advanced close to the desk, dropping his voice.

'She spoke to that Mr Deauville. I couldn't help overhearing. She asked him to go away, and when he said he couldn't, she lost her temper. She threatened him, Miss Lindsay.'

'You're joking, Davies.'

He shook his head. 'I heard her clearly. She said if he didn't go away, you'd be the sufferer.'

'Me! That's a nonsense.'

'I don't think so.'

'What did Philippe say?'

'He was very angry. He said if anyone harmed a hair of your head they'd pay dearly. She was upset. I don't like Her being upset.'

* * *

Barney woke me. He flopped on to the bed and licked my face. Wide spears of sunshine pierced the curtains, highlighting the polished furniture. I guessed it was early, and presumed Felice had let Barney come upstairs. She was probably in the kitchen making tea. I lay for a while, listening for sounds in the house. Soon the silence worried me. Felice was deliberately noisy, she couldn't bear others to be sleeping when she was awake.

Still drowsy, I resented having to get up and see what Felice was doing. I slid out of bed, and pulling on a dressing-gown, ran downstairs. The kitchen was deserted, as was the sitting-room and the studio. The teapot on the kitchen table still felt hot, and I presumed Felice had poured out a cup and taken it back upstairs. But first, perhaps, she may have walked in the garden. The door was not bolted, and I remembered both locking and bolting it before going to bed.

I mounted the stairs to her room. The bedcovers were thrown back, and a pile of clothes were cluttering one chair, just as if she'd rummaged around to find whatever it was she was wearing.

The window was open to its fullest extent. I looked out expecting to see her in the garden. She was not in sight. Well, I thought, if Felice feels the need to go out at five o'clock in the morning, why not?

I still craved sleep. Yesterday had been a long hard day, and I'd experienced too many emotions. Barney had taken possession of my bed. I shuffled in, gently pushing him aside.

Sleep came, but it was the kind of sleep which is too near waking, and the real world intrudes; emotions and problems become the basis of dream-like adventures.

I woke with a start. Barney was growling, and I heard my name being called. I glanced at the bedside clock, and sprang out of bed. I'd be late for work, and too late remembered it was Sunday. I opened my door and called, 'Coming.'

Dora came bouncing up the stairs. 'Lindsay, is Felice with you?'

'Of course not. She's ...' Memory returned. 'Oh my God, hasn't she come back?'

'Back?' Dora's round face creased with puzzlement.

'She went out. Early. She made tea, and went out. At least she must have,' I added lamely.

'You mean you don't know where she is?'

I shook my head. 'I thought she wanted an early morning walk. Maybe paint a dawn picture or something.'

Dora's glance was accusing. 'She was upset. Not herself. I came to make her a cup of tea.' Her face flushed with concern.

'Be a darling, Dora, and make a pot of tea while I get dressed. She'll probably come strolling in any minute now.'

I dragged on jeans and a sweater, and humped Barney off the bed. Dora had made tea and toast by the time I arrived downstairs.

'I'm a worrier,' she said. 'Sit down, love. I shouldn't have woken you. You had a busy day.'

I drank two cups of tea and tackled a piece of buttered toast. Dora's anxiety was communicating itself to me. The fact that she didn't speak was beginning to unnerve me.

'She has no sense of direction,' Dora said at last. 'Once when she was angry with Coniston she was gone a whole day, and he called out the Mountain Rescue.'

'She's selfish and thoughtless.'

'Oh no, Lindsay. She's like a child. She needs

98

to be reassured.'

'And that's my job,' I said grimly.

'Will you ....?'

'Yes, I will,' I rose from the table. 'I'll go and look for her, only God knows what direction to take.'

Dora's relief was ludicrous, but truth to tell, I was nagged with worry myself.

'You stay here, Dora. I'll walk along the top of Gorton Fell and drop down into the village. I'll phone from there, and if she isn't back or I haven't found her, I'll call Roger.'

'That will be best,' Dora said. 'You'll want some food and chocolate and the first aid kit.'

I packed up my haversack, picked up a waterproof, and laced up my climbing boots. Barney was frisking around. I wished he was a bloodhound and could follow Felice's scent; as it was, he was good company.

There were several groups of walkers on Gorton Fell. The well-defined track undulated with the contour of the ground, and on the tops the whole of the valley and the lake became visible. It wasn't a good day for walking, clammy hot, and menacing thunder.

I stopped each small group of walkers, but my enquiries were futile. Felice had been out for nearly five hours, and my anxiety began to mount with every step I took. I'd been keeping a look-out through the field glasses, hoping I would spot her, but no luck, so I took the sheep trod down to the village and telephoned Dora.

Felice hadn't returned. Dora's agitation increased my own fears. Suppose she'd fallen and was lying injured? In a panic I phoned Roger.

'OK. I'll come. I'll bring Davies and the Knight brothers.'

'Oh Roger, thank you.'

'Where are you?'

'Gorton village.'

'Fine. Get yourself a drink in the pub. I'll meet you there.'

The pub doors were open, and I bought an ice-cold shandy and took it outside to sit on the bench and wait for Roger. He was as good as his word. His car pulled up in the pub yard, and Davies and the Knight boys jumped out.

Roger alighted, and put his arms around me and kissed me hard. 'We'll find her, love. No problem.'

Davies was organising the plan of action. He suggested we each took separate paths to the waterfall at Greavey. No way would she go any further than that. High Sail which rose beyond was a place of horror to her.

We agreed to meet back at the pub in an hour and phone Dora. Davies and the Knight boys who were expert climbers, took the high ground to the head of Greavey. Roger traversed the middle ground, and I walked along the path beside the lake, to the spot where the Greavey waters gushed down.

She had been away nearly seven hours, and

my fears were pounding my stomach into a hard lump. Guilt hammered words into my brain—my fault she'd gone off, I hadn't listened or understood. I broke into a run; my heart was racing.

As I approached the waterfall I saw a figure crouched down on the lip on the pool. I called, and Barney pelted toward her, stopping suddenly, as if puzzled. The woman turned her head. It was not my mother. My fears multiplied. Why was she gazing so fixedly into the pool? I raced to her side, and forced myself to look into the water. It was pale green and clear; the light refracted from the white stones in its depths.

'I'm sorry to disturb you,' I said. 'But I'm looking for my mother.'

'You won't find her here,' she said. 'I've been here alone since dawn waiting for a friend. He won't come now or ever.'

Her grief was too deep for further intrusion, and I turned away and walked back to the pub. The landlord recognised me. 'Are you Miss Strong?' I nodded, and he continued, 'Mr Reed left this note for you.'

I tore it open and read. 'Found her, exhausted. Taken her home in the car. Davies and the boys checked in. Walking back. Suggest you wait until I come for you.'

'Thank God,' I said. Relief buckled my legs and I clutched at the landlord.

'There, Miss,' he supported me in his strong

arms, 'no need to take on. I'll get you a good strong cup of tea.'

His arm still round me he led the way into a room behind the bar, Barney following closely. His wife came bustling out of the kitchen.

'Mr Reed's young lady,' he said, guiding me to a chair. 'She's had a bit of shock. Thought her mother was lost on the fells. No need to worry. Mr Reed found her. Grand chap, he is.'

The hot sweet tea revived. I was touched by the kindness of these two good people who seemed to know Roger well. After a little while I felt my strength returning, and with it a slow build up of anger. How dare Felice cause me so much anxiety? I brooded over her behaviour until I heard Roger call my name and went out to meet him. He took my arm, and thanked the landlord and his wife for their kindness, and bundled Barney and me into the car.

'I don't know how to thank you, Roger.'

'Forget it.'

'You came when I needed you.'

'Of course. Now Lindsay, shut up and relax. Felice is fine.' He laughed. 'Quite indignant at being rescued. Nevertheless, she ought to be locked up.' He put the car into gear. 'She'd no right to cause you all this heartache. I told her so.'

He was dependable, and he cared. Was that enough? But as we drove along the narrow roads, a vision of Philippe's face took possession of my mind's eye, and his

102

tantalising smile was like a barb in my heart.

As Roger pulled up at our gate, Dora came rushing out to the car. 'I don't know what to do.' She was twisting her hands together. 'Felice has gone into the studio and locked the door and she won't answer me.'

'Damn the woman,' Roger said, following me through the house to the studio door. He banged on it furiously.

'Let me in at once,' I shouted.

Only quiet in the room. What was she doing?

'If you don't unlock the door now I'll break it down.'

The key turned. I flung open the door. She allowed me in but shut the door in Roger's face, and locked it. She walked back to the easel, ignoring me.

'This is the last time I bother to look for you. I don't care if you never come back.'

'Perhaps that would be best,' she said, standing away from the canvas on the easel. 'I'm a burden to you.' She sighed, and my anger evaporated. I went to her and put my arms round her, kissing her scented cheek. She moved me away gently, and I caught sight of the painting, almost finished; painted, I guessed in a kind of frenzy. The colours were brilliant. High Sail, stark and pitiless, thrust upward to be lost in cloud. In the foreground the house, that phantom house, and a corner of a lake, and at the lake's edge sprawled a man. Dead, I knew he was dead. I stared in sick

103

horror. Had she finally lost her mind? I tightened my arms around her.

She pushed me away. 'So you do care,' she said pettishly. 'I knew you'd come running after me, and you did. Poor Dora was quite hysterical.'

'Why do you do this to us? Davies and the Knight boys are still out on the fell. Why do you want me to feel guilty? Are your sins to be visited on me?'

'Sins,' she shouted the word. 'How stupid you are. Sometimes I think you can't be my daughter. Mine and Con's.'

'You keep me chained to your side. Con escaped . . .'

'How dare you!' She swung round and hit me on the cheek with the flat of her hand.

I turned away, rubbing my face. There would be a red mark and it stung.

'Don't go, Lindsay. I can't bear to be alone. I'm sorry, darling. I didn't mean to hurt you.' She moved my hand and kissed the place. 'There, that'll make it better.'

'No, it won't. You meant to hurt me. All right, I can share your pain if that's what you want. But why are you so disturbed?' I took another look at the canvas. 'I understand your fear of High Sail, but this and this.' I stabbed at the house; and my finger hovered over the body of the dead man.

'No house,' she said. 'No body, only me left.' She began to cry, silently at first, and then in great tearing sobs which shook her body. She had drained me of pity and compassion, but I couldn't just stand there. 'Quiet, quiet,' I soothed, holding her close. I guided her to an armchair, and she leant back, her eyes closed. How young she looked, her fly-away hair falling over her brow. She sighed deeply. 'I'm tired, so tired. I think I'll go to bed.'

I accompanied her upstairs; turned down the bed, drew the curtains.

'You won't go away,' she said anxiously. 'I mean, you'll stay in the house.'

'Of course. I'll look in on you later.'

I needed a drink; Davies was in the kitchen making tea.

'Gin,' I said. 'A double. How about you?'

He nodded and abandoned the teapot, and accepted a glass of whisky.

'Where's Roger?'

'He rushed off. He was raging. He doesn't understand Her.'

'I don't think I do, either. She makes me feel afraid, helpless.' I spread my hands out on the table and he covered them.

'Come into the studio. I want to show you something.' He finished his drink, and followed me into the room.

'Look at this,' I stood before the easel. 'I can understand her obsession with High Sail, but I don't understand the significance of this and this.' I pointed to the house and the body of the man.

He stared at it for a moment and then turned away and walked out of the house. He was breathing quickly, as if he'd run a long way. He sat down on the white painted garden seat, and I sat beside him.

'Is that house imagination?' I persisted. 'Whose body is that supposed to be?'

'Imagination. Hers. Her dreams.'

'More like nightmares. Come, Davies, that answer won't do.'

'She'll speak in her own good time.' He stood up and patted me on the shoulder. I guessed he'd say no more. I watched him stride down the path, and heard the sound his studded boots made in the lane long after he was out of sight.

I returned to the studio and took the canvas off the easel, and hid it among other pictures stacked against the wall.

Perhaps, I thought, when she wakes she'll forget she's painted it. But I wouldn't. I would return to it again and again. It was the shadow in her life and mine.

CHAPTER EIGHT

'This letter arrived yesterday.' Philippe and I sat in the cocktail bar in the Lake End Hotel. 'It was addressed to my mother, and the Deauville lawyers forwarded it on to me.' His eyes sparkled, and he impatiently pushed strands of hair back from his forehead.

'It's from a firm of solicitors in Chester. An old Aunt of my mother's has just died. She was my grandmother's sister. The letter asked my mother to get in touch with them.'

'Chester,' I said reflectively.

'I telephoned and it was suggested I called to see them. At the same time I was given the name and address of a cousin.'

'So you were looking in the wrong place.' I wasn't sure if I was thankful or not. Philippe's departure would probably hasten Felice's recovery, but the thought of him being beyond my reach was like an ice-pack round my heart.

'This cousin has invited me for the weekend and suggested I brought a friend. Will you come with me, Lindsay?'

His eagerness was flattering. I wanted desperately to be with him, but wouldn't it make an eventual parting more painful?

'I'd like to, but ...'

'I know,' he said impatiently, 'Felice won't let you out of her sight.'

Put like that it sounded as if I was a prisoner, and priggish.

'I'll come,' I said quickly, as if I was making a momentous decision.

He smiled and my heart squirmed.

'I knew you would, Lindsay. You don't let people down.'

I laughed. 'But I am. I mean Roger is going

107

to hit the roof, and Felice ...'

'Is she better?'

'I don't know, Philippe. She's crawled into a cocoon. I can't reach her. God knows what I'd do if Dora wasn't so devoted. Felice has rejected me, and I don't know why.'

I hadn't meant to show Philippe or anyone else the despair which was corroding the days.

'Come on, Lindsay,' he said briskly. 'What you need is food and wine, and someone to coddle you.' He took my arm and we walked into the dining-room. A waiter rushed forward to seat us at a table. Philippe consulted me over the menu, the waiter made helpful suggestions and eventually brought the starters.

'This letter has changed so much.' Philippe dug into his slice of melon. 'It's like entering an uncharted country. The two halves of my being will come together. If I don't find out who is my father, I shall feel cheated for the rest of my life.'

'Philippe, don't get too hopeful. I mean suppose your cousin believes you really are a Deauville.'

And that was exactly the situation we found on our arrival at The Gables.

The drive to Chester was uneventful, but sitting close to Philippe I was aware of his rising excitement, which bubbled over as we drew up before the impressive front door. The Gables was on the outskirts of the city, a traditional black and white Cheshire house, in

108

large grounds sloping down to the River Dee.

Mrs Cornell, Barbara, met us at the door. She was tall and elegant, and greeted Philippe with a smile which refused to melt the frosty look in her eyes. She shook hands, invited us into the hall, and showed us to our rooms.

When we descended the stairs she was waiting in the hall and we followed her into the drawing-room, all antique furniture, and set pieces of arranged flowers.

'My husband will be late as usual.' She offered us sherry. 'He plays golf all weekend. Very frustrating. Do you play, Philippe?'

'Afraid not,' Philippe said easily. 'My besetting passion is cricket.'

William Cornell blustered in as we were drinking a third sherry. 'Sorry love.' He tried to kiss an adroitly turned cheek. 'Glad to meet you both. More sherry?' He picked up the bottle and proceeded to fill up our glasses, and poured himself a large one, despite his wife's frown. Red veins criss-crossed his weather-beaten face, and his bright blue eyes twinkled with amusement.

'Lunch is ready.' Barbara led the way into the dining-room, and placed us round a table set with lace mats, and a centrepiece of roses in a silver vase.

William brought up the rear, clutching his glass. Barbara served the salmon, caught locally she informed. William poured the wine, and when he eventually sat down he leaned towards Philippe.

'You favour Eve,' he said. 'She was a looker. The beauty of the family.'

This remark didn't go down well with Barbara. She became frostier than ever.

'Did you know my mother?' he asked eagerly.

'Who didn't?' William's laugh was infectious. 'She had every lad in the city mad for her. And she was clever. She read languages at Liverpool University. Spoke French like a native. And she adored animals. Never without a dog or cat.'

Philippe smiled. 'That's right. She had numberless poodles. Bred them much to father's annoyance. She hated to part with the puppies.'

'And she loved horses,' William continued. 'She rode like a trooper, eh Barbara?'

Barbara nodded. I doubted she'd had much affection for the girl her husband had obviously admired. Had she, Barbara, been second choice? Eve Deauville was emerging from the shadows. I'd thought of her as a secret person, plain perhaps, thankfully marrying André Deauville, ten years her senior for the sake of her son.

'I bet you have plenty of horses in the Deauville stables,' William said.

'That's right. The Deauville racing colours are well known in France and England. My mother taught us all to ride.'

'Eve was never far away from the local riding stables when she lived here.'

'Here?' Philippe looked surprised.

'Didn't you know?' William said. 'I thought ...' he looked questioningly at his wife, but she remained silent, so he continued, 'Eve came to live here with Barbara's family after her father was killed in the war. Great fellow, your grandfather, Philippe. He flew a Spitfire, one of the "Few." Eve's mother was killed shortly after in an air raid.'

'This house has always been my home.' Barbara glanced at her husband. 'Naturally we had Eve to live with us.'

'Barbara and I married during the war. I was in the Navy. And when I was demobbed, I couldn't get a job. So we lived here, thought it best at the time, and here we've stayed.'

'It's a lovely house,' I said. 'I'm longing to explore the garden.'

'I've done a good job there,' William said proudly. 'I wanted to be a gardener—hated the city—but eventually the family fixed up a job in insurance in Manchester. Never took to it,' he added.

'William bores everyone with his gardening exploits,' Barbara said. 'I'm sure you aren't interested, Miss Strong.'

'Oh but I am. I look after our garden, but I'm not an expert. Perhaps you'll give me some tips, Mr Cornell?'

He smiled. 'Delighted. Call me William,

111

easier.'

Neither Philippe or Barbara accompanied us into the garden. The great aunt had willed Philippe's mother some treasured possessions, and Barbara suggested they sorted out the articles he'd like to keep. I was glad to escape her antagonism.

'The wife's upset,' William confided, as we admired a wonderful display of roses. 'She was fond of her great aunt.'

I didn't think the death of the old lady was the cause of Barbara's coldness towards us. I was pretty sure she resented Philippe because he was Eve's son, and William's next words confirmed my supposition.

'Philippe seems a nice chap. I understand Eve had quite a brood.' I recognised the envy and longing in his voice.

'Philippe has three brothers,' I said, as we wandered through the herb garden; the mingling scents filling me with nostalgia.

'Lucky fellow,' William muttered, and I guessed he meant André Deauville.

We passed under an archway on which great mauve racemes of wistaria hung, and arrived at a seat on the bank of the river, and sat down.

'It was a shock to hear Eve was dead.' He offered me a cigarette and took one himself. 'I often used to think about her. Always thought she'd marry one of the crowd. You'll meet some of them. Barbara has asked them in for drinks to meet Philippe. But no, she cleared off

112

to France. I think her holiday in the Lake District unsettled her. And the next thing we hear is she's married to Deauville.'

My heart sank. 'Did she have friends in the Lake District?'

He nodded. 'Lass she was friendly with at the University. Odd girl, very striking, black hair, glowing eyes, very intense.'

'Do you remember her name?'

He looked at me curiously and hesitated. 'Can't say I do. All I can remember is she was Irish, and wrote poetry.'

'But did she live in the Lake District?' I persisted.

'Don't think so. The girls stayed around in youth hostels. Though I do remember Eve was pally with an artist.'

'Artist?' I repeated stupidly.

'Yes, a talented girl apparently. She gave Eve some pictures. Eve took two away with her, and left one here. I liked it so she gave it to me and it is still hanging in my den.' He laughed rumbustiously. 'Den—sounds as if I'm a bear. Eve used to call me the biggest and best bear she was ever likely to meet.'

'Did you care a lot for her?' I asked softly.

'Oh yes, I loved her,' he said simply. 'But you see it was too late.' He patted my shoulder, and his mouth slackened, his eyes moistened; living another time. And I wondered if he could possibly be Philippe's father, but dismissed the thought instantly.

'She never knew how much I cared,' he went on. 'She went away in the spring, and stayed up in the Lake District with her friends all summer. It was October when she came back to collect her belongings, and she didn't even stay the night.'

That far-off summer had suddenly come near and into focus. I imagined Eve and her striking Irish friend, and Felice, for I had no doubt my mother was the third member of that carefree trio. So what had happened?

William's voice brought me back to the present. 'How did you meet Philippe?' he asked.

'I work in the Reed Gallery in Longmere. Philippe came in to buy a picture,' I said easily.

'The wife doesn't like pictures. She goes in for all those blasted china figures. I'm afraid to move sometimes,' he grumbled.

I was getting to like William very much, and Barbara a lot less.

'Come and see my asparagus plot.' We weaved along the slender sandy paths into the vegetable garden. 'I grow all our own vegetables. Barbara thinks I ought to get a gardener—like the neighbours.' He laughed again, but this time I heard a note of anger, a hurt unhealed.

We sauntered through the vegetable patch, and I told him how Coniston had had the great idea of planting Christmas trees and selling them in due course. But he could never bear to

114

uproot them, and now they flourished as a memorial to him.

'Sensible man,' William said. 'See those willows. Barbara wants them cut down. Won't agree. She does what she likes in the house, but the garden is mine,' he added fiercely.

The picture hanging in William's den was, as I'd suspected, one of Felice's. Only it was totally unlike the ones Philippe owned. The portion of the lake, the reedy bank, and the golden blur of daffodils gave a feeling of happiness. The mountains behind were shadows, not clearly defined; clouds misting the summits. And on the lake a boat—empty.

'Funny thing about that boat,' William said. 'Abandoned, not moored or anything, as if . . .' He paused, a puzzled frown wrinkling his brow. 'I asked Eve about it, and she just said keep the picture for me. One day I might want to remember. Very odd I thought at the time. Still do. And now she's dead,' he sighed gustily. 'Do you think Philippe will mind if I keep it—in remembrance?'

William mentioned the picture to Philippe as we sipped china tea and ate thin crustless cucumber sandwiches in the drawing-room. Philippe's gut reaction to the picture was the same as mine. Felice was the key to the mystery, and she wasn't talking.

The Cornells' friends arrived for drinks. It was obvious they were a 'crowd'. Long standing relationships, thrusting back into the

115

past. I tried to imagine which of these well-heeled city gents had fancied Eve. Their recollections of her were guarded; the wives slightly resentful, the husbands regretful. Philippe impressed them because they respected money, possessions and power. And Eve, by marrying into the Deauville family had become in their eyes, a success beyond their expectations.

Philippe came to my room early the following morning. I was dressed and watching the mist lift steadily from the river.

He put his arms round me and kissed me. 'Let's push off early. We can have the whole day to ourselves.'

'Won't the Cornells be offended?'

'I suppose so.' He leant out of the open window. 'I can't stand this house, it stifles me. No wonder my mother didn't hang about.' He stared fixedly into the garden. 'Do you think William ...?'

'Certainly not,' I interrupted. 'Eve's love wasn't here.'

He sighed with relief. 'I began to fear horrible complications.'

'You could do worse than William,' I said.

'I think that's what I'm afraid of. Suppose ...' he paused.

'Leave it, Philippe. I think you are worrying unnecessarily. You are you, and who cares about your parents.'

'I do,' he said soberly. 'That picture William

116

dotes on, typifies how I feel. An empty vessel, floating with the current. And somewhere out of reach a golden future. Do you think Felice was trying to say something?'

'Yes, I do. But not the sort of thing you're imagining. I think something traumatic happened when she met Eve, something Felice wants to forget, and maybe Eve thrust the same thing down below her subconscious, because she never talked to you about the past.'

'I guess you're right. Pack your bag, love, and let's see if we can make an early getaway.'

Barbara would have been glad to see the back of us as soon as we'd obliged her by praising the good old English breakfast which neither Philippe or I appreciated.

William, however, was not going to allow us to escape so easily. He had cancelled a morning's golf, a great sacrifice, and he wasn't going to be left to moon around under his wife's eye. He suggested a visit to a nearby garden centre. Barbara was scornful.

'For heaven's sake, William, take them on the river, and we can meet for drinks with the crowd.'

'We'd love to go to the garden centre,' I said hastily, and Philippe agreed, stipulating that we'd like to leave after an early lunch.

William was in his element at the Rightway Garden Centre. He was greeted familiarly by the staff, and let us into his big secret, carefully concealed from Barbara, that he was part owner, and had lined up a happy retirement for himself.

He insisted on presenting me with a special rose tree. A hybrid he'd grown, and named 'Eve'. It was a pale pink deepening to a clear red on the edges of the petals. Philippe was enchanted, and bought half a dozen, which he intended to be planted in the Deauville Gardens, if and when they could be exported.

We took our departure as soon as politeness permitted, and drove out of the wrought iron gates with sighs of relief.

'Thank you,' Philippe said. 'I didn't know what I was letting you in for. I'm afraid the weekend wasn't much of a success.'

'Nonsense,' I said. 'I've enjoyed meeting William, and I've discovered Eve.'

I didn't say that the fact of spending the time with him was the source of my enjoyment. If only Philippe would abandon his quest for his wretched father, I was sure we'd draw closer still.

'William suggested we might like to have tea at some riverside café. Another of his secret projects I suspect. He gave me explicit directions and told me to be sure and mention his name.'

'Why not? He really is a dear.'

'Poor William, he confided in me he'd sling his hook as he put it, if it wasn't for his garden. I wonder if Barbara made my mother unhappy? Perhaps that's why she left, went

118

north, and then to France. I wish I'd questioned her, but I never thought about her life before she married into the Deauville family.'

'I can understand that. I think Eve was a private person. She's suddenly become real to me.'

He smiled, delighted. 'I wish you two had met.'

We turned into a narrow lane; arched trees cast dappled shadows. Beyond the hedges cattle sought shade, and like a thread of light the river pointed the way.

Riverside Tea Gardens were at the end of the lane. Brightly coloured umbrellas shaded tables set on a worn lawn. We chose a table at the water's edge, and a young woman came out of the converted cottage to take our order.

Philippe mentioned William's name, and a roguish gleam lit up the woman's eyes. 'Ah, there's a man,' she said, and then defiantly added, 'he's our friend.'

'No wonder William enjoys this place,' I said, idly watching the river's smooth liquid movement disturbed by the rising fish. 'His secret place,' I said. 'We all need one.'

And mine; where was mine? The Greavey waterfall, I thought, where the silence was only broken by the splash of water on rocks, and the curlew's mournful cry; and there was no past and no present in the unchanging vistas.

An elderly lady arrived and sat down at a

table in the shade. A young woman herded before her three children, two boys and a girl. I watched the children, listening to Philippe explain the ramifications of his family. The boys were quarrelling. The mother yelled at them, and then wandered away to the café to order tea. The little girl climbed down from her chair and endeavoured to stop the boys punching each other.

Philippe turned his back on them. 'Let's go,' he said abruptly, feeling in his pocket for his wallet. 'Damn, I must have dropped it in the car or left it at The Gables. I'd better phone.' He sprang up, and walked away in the direction of the car-park.

The little girl was crying. She had silver fair hair, caught up on either side of her face with two glittering slides. She tried to insinuate herself between her brothers. I wished their mother would return; the little peacemaker was so desperately ineffectual. I pushed back my chair ready to intervene.

'Stop it!' I shouted.

The boys ignored me, but the girl turned, and unexpectedly caught off balance, either tripped or was pushed into the river.

There was a momentous silence. I sprang up, kicked off my shoes and jumped into the river. I saw the glitter of her bright slides beneath the surface of the water and grabbed her. Her body was tense with fright, and she clung to me with surprising strength.

120

'You're safe.' I held her head above the water which was not deep, and paddled back to the bank. The elderly lady loomed above me, and I passed the child up to her. She ordered the boys to fetch their mother. I tried to clamber up the bank, but my feet were held fast in the mud. Every move I made, I sank deeper.

'Get help,' I shouted. 'I'm stuck in the mud.'

The woman laid the child down and disappeared. I grasped at the coarse grasses and reeds, but they broke away in my hands. It was quiet; so quiet, I was conscious of my thumping heart, and for a frightful second I had a vision of Felice's last picture; and a dead body on the bank.

Philippe's voice killed thought. He knelt on the bank, arms outstretched. Our fingers touched; he leant further, and grasped my hands. 'Hold on, Lindsay, for God's sake, hold on.'

He was pulling, firmly, but all I could think was the mud was tightening its grip, and I'd never be free. He was pulling harder now, so hard I thought my arms would come out of the sockets; and suddenly with a horrible squelch my legs came free, and I was sprawling on the bank beside him.

'Lindsay, oh darling Lindsay.' His hands still gripped mine, and I couldn't bear to loosen my hold.

The café staff came belting across the grass, anxiously standing around. 'Is she hurt?'

'I'm fine, except I stink. How's the little girl?'
'She's OK.'

Philippe stood up and lifted me into his arms.

'I think a hot bath is the answer,' he said carrying me to the café.

I was escorted up the stairs into a super modern bathroom. Hot water gushed into the bath, scented soap and bath salts were offered. Philippe fetched my case from the car, and I dressed in dry clothes.

When I descended the stairs, Philippe was waiting. He caught me in his arms, holding me so close I could hardly breathe. He cared; maybe he loved me, and maybe he didn't, but at least he cared.

He settled me in the car, and we drove some way in silence.

'Don't mention this to Felice,' I said.

He drew up in a lay-by, and switched off the engine, capturing my hand. 'Why not?'

'I'm not sure. Water is part of her fear. When Roger found her and brought her back from the fell, she shut herself up in the studio and painted a frightening picture.' I shivered.

'Why didn't you tell me?' he demanded.

'I showed it to Davies. He didn't say anything; but his face whitened, and he was so upset he rushed out of the house. I hid it.'

'Why?'

I shivered again. 'There was so much menace in it. The lake, an empty boat, a body.'

He put his arms round me. 'Don't think about it.'

I felt his lips on my brow, my cheeks, my neck. 'Oh my God, Lindsay,' he muttered, 'if anything had happened to you.'

I waited, hoping for more, but in a moment he released me and I knew he wouldn't say any more; he'd go away, and I'd lose him, if he didn't discover the name of his father.

CHAPTER NINE

'I'm leaving.' Jenna wheeled herself into the office and banged the door behind her.

I looked up from the welter of papers on the desk. 'Leaving?' I repeated vaguely. 'Do you mean now?'

'Of course I don't.' She hammered the arms of her chair as if to gain my full attention. 'The doctor at the hospital has arranged for me to go to a clinic in Hungary. He thinks there may be a chance of regaining the use of my legs.'

'That's splendid. I do hope so Jenna.'

'Of course you do. I'll stop being a burden to Roger. He'll be free.'

'I'm sure Roger ...'

'Oh don't flannel me, Lindsay. You know exactly how Roger feels. He's been great. But I want my independence. I want a separate life from his.' She flung out her arms in an embracing gesture. Her eyes were shining; she was so alive in her useless body. All my dislike of her melted and drained away for the first time since Coniston's death.

She was regarding me with an unusually serious expression. 'Lindsay, you probably know the terms of my old man's Will; Roger discusses them endlessly. Well, I'm pulling out. I mean, I'm resigning. I'm withdrawing my share of the capital.'

'Does this mean Roger will have to sell the Gallery?'

'Of course not, stupid. Do you really think I'd do that to him?'

'No.' I was confused. 'I'm sure you wouldn't harm him.'

'You're dead right, I wouldn't. The old man left contingency plans in case I married.' She grimaced. 'Dick Outhwaite is one of the trustees. He's agreed to release part of the trust fund to keep the Gallery solvent. I need my share if I'm going to Hungary. It won't be cheap. But there is something else. I have to be replaced—a new partner for Roger.' She paused, and grasped the arms of her chair so tightly, her knuckles shone white. 'You.'

It was all happening the way I'd felt was right. I'd worked so hard at making the Gallery a success, but always I had to wait for the approval of Roger and Jenna. But now it had changed—there was Philippe. Dare I allow my love for Philippe to stand in the way of ambition?

'You don't have to answer me,' Jenna said quickly. 'Roger will be furious I've spoken to you, but I thought it only fair you should have warning and a chance to think about it. I mean you and Roger—oh hell, Lindsay, you must know how he feels about you.'

'Do I?' I said quietly. 'Roger and I are friends . . .'

She interrupted, 'And you could be lovers if you wanted. He needs you, Lindsay. I hate to say it, but it's true. He really needs you.'

Was need enough? I wondered, and doubted.

'And there's another thing I've got to say, just in case anything goes wrong.' Her lips trembled, and her eyes misted over. 'My chances are only fifty-fifty. I want you to know the truth about Coniston's death. Ask Dick Outhwaite, he witnessed it. He was there.' She scrubbed her eyes with an impatient gesture. 'I'd like to part friends.'

I jumped up and kissed her cheek.

'Thanks, Lindsay. You won't ever get the truth out of Felice. She's a will of iron under that silly feminine exterior. She only believes what suits her. It's up to you, if you want to know the truth. Now be a love, and open this damned door for me.'

I watched her propel herself at speed down the Gallery, shouting to Davies to open the main doors. I sat down at the desk and stared

125

into the future. Did I really have a choice? Did Felice's seeming helplessness influence me to a duty toward her?

How could I let Roger down? I knew he needed me, and why not, we were friends, colleagues, and if he was to be believed his intention was marriage.

Against all this, how could I set this raging love for Philippe, unrequited, and likely to remain so? For all I knew he might have other commitments. Certainly he'd told me of his broken engagement, but that didn't mean there wasn't another woman tucked away somewhere.

I sighed, and tried to concentrate on my work, but found myself gazing into space. How would I answer Roger? Who could I go to for advice? At least I had a breathing space. Roger was away and I didn't expect him back for a few days.

I left the Gallery early, promising myself I'd make up for lost time the next day. I felt shivery, and supposed the shock of being stuck in the cold river water the previous day was beginning to take effect. However, by the time I reached home I felt better, and decided to take Barney a walk on the fells.

The walk to Greavey and a rest by the waterfall restored me to normality. When I arrived back, Dora was in the kitchen.

'Where's Felice?' I asked.

'Headache. She's asleep. Come home with

me, I've just fixed a meal.'

She made me comfortable in a deep chintz covered chair, and put a glass of sherry in my hand. 'Relax, my dear. You are all tensed up.'

I sipped my drink gratefully. Dora set the finishing touches to the table, and when all was ready ushered me to a seat. The room was so peaceful, so bright with its white walls in contrast to the oak beams, and well-worn furniture. It was a real home.

'Tell me about your weekend?' she demanded.

She was interested in the Cornells, the house, their friends, and the garden, and most of all in the picture William owned.

'Describe it,' she said.

I did so.

'I remember it. A happy picture would you say?'

'In a way. Except for the empty boat. Why does Felice go on painting empty boats?'

Dora jumped up. We had rounded off our meal with one of Dora's special concoctions, wickedly rich. 'Sit here love,' she plumped up the cushions in an easy chair, 'and don't move. I'll just slip next door and see if Felice is awake and if she wants anything.'

I sat down, and relaxed. No wonder Dora was good for Felice; she had such a contented nature. I closed my eyes and dozed. When I came to, Dora was pouring coffee. 'Philippe phoned while I was fixing Felice a drink. He told me about your courageous action in rescuing the little girl. He's on his way here.'

'It was a natural reaction,' I said. 'Did you tell Felice?'

'No. Philippe insisted I shouldn't. Lindsay, do you realise she is jealous of him. She is reconciled to the idea that she may lose you one day to Roger. But she knows that both you and Roger would continue to look after her.'

'She has you,' the words were spoken before I'd time to think.

'Second best.' Dora flushed. 'I've always been second best. Even my husband married me on the rebound.'

'I'm sure that's not true.'

'Perhaps I cheated, because for me he was second best too. I was in love with Leslie Outhwaite. We all were, me, Felice, and other girls too.'

'Isn't Leslie a nephew of Dick's? Who was the lucky winner?'

'No one. He died.'

I dismissed Leslie Outhwaite as a distant figure from the past.

'And where does my father fit into this picture?'

Dora grinned. 'You know what Con was like. A whirlwind courtship and marriage. He was desperately in love with Felice.' She paused. 'Felice loved him, you know, and she was utterly loyal. She needed support, and Con gave her that. He believed in her talent.'

She wasn't telling me anything new, I was well aware of how Felice and Con had felt about each other.

Philippe's arrival cut short any further reminiscences. She dashed off to the kitchen for more coffee, leaving us alone.

'I was worried.' He bent down and kissed me lightly on the cheek. 'You haven't caught cold?'

'Of course not. I felt tired, and Dora has been spoiling me,' I said, as she returned with the coffee-pot.

'I think I'll just look in on Felice again,' she said coyly.

Philippe grinned. 'The ever tactful Dora. Where is Felice?'

'Lying down. She has a headache.'

He looked at me thoughtfully. 'Would that be her little protest? Our happy weekend and all that?'

'Not fair,' I said without conviction. Because of course, that was exactly what it was.

He drank his coffee, and helped himself to more. 'Jenna asked me to accompany her to Hungary to the clinic. She made quite a fuss when I refused.'

'She'll make it. She always has.'

'I don't think she believed me when I pleaded a trip to London. But in any case, I'm sure Roger would want to take her.'

'Would you have liked to go?'

He looked away. 'It seemed like a kindness . . .'

'Kindness,' I exploded. 'Jenna doesn't look for kindness. She needs attention, admiration, love, total devotion.'

'So do most women,' he said huffily. 'It's a pity you two aren't friends. She needs a woman.'

'Well,' I conceded, 'we have come to an understanding.'

'That's good.' He leaned forward enthusiastically. 'She's in a rotten position. The accident ruined her life.'

'And killed my father.'

He stood up. 'Do you feel like a walk down to the lake? I want to take some photos.'

'If you like,' I replied indifferently. He seemed utterly lost to me, his thoughts occupied with Jenna's predicament.

'I do like, my sweet Lindsay.' He put out his hands and drew me to my feet, holding me tenderly close for a moment.

Down by the lake there was a breeze. The water was ruffled; white cuffs breaking against the banks.

Philippe fiddled with his camera, moving from point to point; standing, sitting, lying.

'Are you entering a competition or something?'

'It's the light. Felice paints this kind of evening light and it's magical. She's a genius.'

'No, she isn't. She's just a good artist, and difficult to live with.'

He crouched down at the water's edge, the camera focused directly in front of him. The water's surface had a silver sheen, points of light picked up by the slight movement. And across on the other bank a house, partly hidden by garden foliage, heightened the unreality of the scene. For a second in the uncertain light I thought I glimpsed the shape of Felice's mysterious house.

Philippe stood up. 'It must be a trick of the light. That house ...'

'You mean the middle one almost hidden by trees? For a second I thought it looked like Felice's dream house. Take a photo,' I commanded. I studied the house, and realised I knew it well.

'I don't believe it, Philippe.' I joined him at the water's edge. 'Guess who owns that house? The Outhwaites.' And at that moment a man appeared on the short jetty, unmoored the boat, and set a course across the lake directly towards us. He shut off the motor, and the boat bumped gently against the bank.

'Thought it was you,' he called. 'Come over for a drink.'

'How on earth could you recognise us?' I asked, as we clambered aboard.

Dick Outhwaite laughed. 'A little secret. We have a telescope.'

He started up the motor as soon as we were seated, and carried us swiftly across. Peggy was waiting on the jetty. She flung her arms round me as I climbed out. 'Lindsay darling, how absolutely lovely to see you. And Philippe. I said to Dick, didn't I? Those two young people must be longing for a drink.' She led the way back to the terrace. 'Philippe, are you good at barbecues? Dick says we are behind the times because we resisted buying one, and now we've got it, we don't use it.'

'Lead me to it.'

Philippe's expertise was a pleasure to watch, and soon the aroma of frying Cumberland sausages filled the air.

I wandered down to the lake's edge, still deeply disturbed by the fleeting vision of the Outhwaites' house from the other bank. From this side, there was a familiarity of line, which I now realised figured in many of Felice's pictures.

Dick joined me. 'I never tire of this view.'

'Felice often painted it, didn't she?'

'Yes, in the early days, before she married Coniston.'

'How did you meet her?'

'My nephew was at the same Art College. He brought her here.'

'Leslie?' I queried.

'Yes,' Dick sighed. 'He's dead. Poor Leslie, such talent and such a stupid accident.'

'What happened?'

'He drowned in this lake.' He turned away. 'Come on, Lindsay, the sausages will be ready.'

Drowned in this lake; the phrase spun round and round in my head as we settled in cushioned chairs on the terrace. The sausages were rich and spicy, and Peggy offered crusty bread and pickles to go with them.

The lake was drawing on its evening cloak. That indefinable colour of blue-grey that Felice captured with heart-catching success. And as we ate and sipped wine, a rowing boat pulled out from the other shore, and anchored in the centre. The lone figure cast out a line and sat motionless in the prow.

Leslie. Drowned in this lake. How? Not a lake to be feared. No hidden currents; no great deeps, and only stirred to violence in the sudden storms which occasionally blew up. But even so, there would have been time to reach the jetty.

I don't know why this long ago tragedy affected me; but it appeared like a vivid scene which might have been enacted before my eyes. And suddenly I knew why. I had seen it all before in so many of Felice's pictures. I glanced at Philippe; he was looking round uneasily.

Dick touched my arm. 'Jenna phoned. This Hungary business. Is it wise?'

'I suppose if it gives her a chance of walking again, it's worth it.'

'And if it doesn't?'

'I don't know how she'll live with it. Dick,

she says you saw the climbing accident. How?'

He looked away. Peggy interposed, 'We don't know what happened.'

'I think you do,' I said quietly. 'Coniston was your best friend. Did you cover up for him?'

Peggy gasped. Her face blotched with anger. 'How dare you say such a thing, Lindsay. Your own father ...'

'That's why. I need to know the truth.'

Dick said angrily. 'Forget it. It's in the past.'

'Not for Jenna, it isn't. You see, all I know is hearsay. An account from you Dick. Telling me nothing. I have a right to know the truth.' I appealed to Philippe, 'Isn't that so?'

'Better let it go,' he said quietly.

'Come off it Philippe. You've no intention of letting go of your problem. It isn't fair to Jenna. Felice has hated her ever since. She blames the girl for the accident, and when I press Felice she dissolves into tears.'

'I didn't see the accident.' Peggy's hurried words only heightened my suspicions.

'Felice may not have seen the accident, but it haunts her,' I said quietly. 'She paints High Sail as if in a nightmare, just as she paints this lake and an empty boat.'

'Nonsense,' the Outhwaites said together.

I shook my head. 'Remember Con used to take me climbing on the easy faces? I haven't forgotten his tactics. He knew the mountain was an adversary. So, up on that almost unclimbable face he and Jenna must have roped up. If he fell Jenna may not have had the strength to hold him. He was killed and Jenna badly injured. So what went wrong?'

Dick stood up. He was very angry. 'This is ridiculous, and wholly unnecessary. I'm sure Felice told you ...'

I interrupted. 'She has never spoken of the accident to me. I presumed as do others that it was Jenna's fault. Now I want to know what actually happened, Dick.'

Dick sat down, covering his face with his hands. When at last he looked up, I was stricken by the misery in his eyes.

'Lindsay is right. It's been long on my conscience that I didn't set the record straight.'

Peggy flared up. 'We agreed, Dick. We can't go back on a promise to Felice now. It will break her heart.'

'What about Jenna? Young, beautiful, condemned to a wheelchair. You've let me and others believe she was to blame, because Felice can't bear Con's image should be tarnished.'

Peggy leapt to her feet, and stood over me. 'We won't listen to you, will we Dick? Tell her, it's finished, and it's none of her business.'

'Well Dick? Can you tell me my father's death is none of my business?'

Dick leaned forward, placing his hands on my knees.

'Lindsay, I beg of you, forget it. There was an accident, and that's the truth.'

135

'Then if it was an accident as you say, why has Felice pinned all the blame on to Jenna? You have never told me the circumstances of this accident, and when I came home Felice was in no state to be questioned. I have been wrong, I should have asked for the truth before. But until Jenna said you saw the accident, I didn't wish to upset Felice. But the situation is changed. Jenna is right. I want to know the truth.'

Dick stood up. 'I asked Felice if I could tell you how it happened, but she made me promise. I have to break that promise now.' He walked away to the house, with the gait and steps of an old man.

Tears filled my eyes, and dripped heedlessly down my cheeks.

'Oh God, Philippe what have I done?'

He pulled me close, and kissed my hair, my eyes, my wet cheeks: passionless kisses bestowed on a hurt child, to soothe the pain.

In a little while Dick returned. 'Take this.' He thrust a diary into my hand. 'My account of the accident, and it is only my version.'

'Dick, are you sure you want me to read it?'

'Yes,' he said firmly. 'Peggy doesn't agree with me; she's quite upset. If you don't mind, I'll take you back across the lake.'

We boarded the boat and he started up the motor, and bore us swiftly across to the other bank.

'Dick?' I touched his arm as we alighted.

'You're right,' he said gruffly. 'Only I beg of you don't let Felice know I've lent you my diary. If she is to find a semblance of peace, she can only do so as long as she keeps her illusions.'

*　　*　　*

'I think I've lost two friends.' I hugged the diary to my breast.

'Their loyalty has always been to Felice.' Philippe took my arm and we turned away from the lake and began to walk up the path to the lane. The light was beginning to fade.

'I have to know, Philippe. Not knowing, excludes me.'

'She will not forgive you.'

I didn't need him to speak her name. She had paid dearly for her illusions, and she wouldn't let them go cheaply.

At the gate of our cottage he left me, suggesting no future meetings. I was overwhelmed with sadness. I clutched the hard cover of Dick's diary so tightly it made a ridge on my hands. Should I turn back and throw it in the lake unread? And if I did, what then?

There were no lights showing in our cottage, but Dora's sitting-room was illuminated, and I presumed that Felice, cured of her headache was keeping Dora company.

Barney barked as I turned the key in the lock and pelted out as I opened the door. He stood on the path waiting for his usual walk; no way could I disappoint him. But first I took the diary to my room and locked it in a drawer.

Barney led the way on to the fell. The distant mountains were mauve, slowly blending with the night sky. Dusk dropped quickly now, and all I could see was the glimmer of the track. I walked slowly, composing my mind. I needed to believe that what I was about to do was right.

When I at last returned, Dora's cottage was in darkness, and a light showed in Felice's bedroom. I ran up the stairs.

'Is your headache better?'

She was sitting up in bed, reading. 'Yes, thanks to Dora,' she said pointedly. 'I do wish you wouldn't take that dog out so late. Something dreadful might happen to you.'

She put the book and her reading spectacles on the bedside table, and snuggled down under the covers. 'Dora and I have been making fudge for the church fête. I'm helping her on the sweet stall.'

I bent and kissed her soft cheek. 'Sleep well.' I shut her door and entered my room. Bathing my face with cold water, I undressed quickly, and putting on my housecoat sat at the desk to read Dick's diary.

A ribbon marker indicated the page where he wished me to open it. The date at the top of the page was 4th May. Dick's crabbed handwriting needed concentration. Here was a

138

lawyer writing a factual report. He was stating facts, without comment or bias.

He wrote: *Terrible day. Coniston killed on High Sail. Jenna seriously injured. Low cloud, and melting snow in the crevices. North face wet. Accompanied them across the screes to the foot of the rock. Damn dangerous in these conditions. Pleaded with Con to abandon the climb for Felice's sake. He said they'd quarrelled over Jenna's stupid challenge. Roped up. Coniston lead. Tapped in pitons at intervals. Belayed the rope. Jenna climbing to right of him. Searched for holds in a deep fissure. Con holding her by the rope. Slow progress. Could see they were having difficulties. Con didn't see the lump of rock hurtling down, caught him on the shoulder. Knocked him off his stance. He fell thirty or forty feet on the rope. An overhang broke his fall. I couldn't see him moving. Jenna began the descent. Lost her foothold in her haste. Fell on to the same ledge as Con. Without proper gear I couldn't reach them. Scrambled down to the road and car. Drove to the nearest telephone and called out the police and Mountain Rescue. A very tricky rescue. At last it was completed. Con was dead when they brought him down, Jenna unconscious. I followed the ambulance to the hospital.*

I don't know how I will find the courage to tell Felice.

Here the entry ended. I turned the pages, and saw the next entry was Dick had telephoned me to come home.

At the bottom of the next page he had written that he had attended the Inquest and the verdict on Coniston was accidental death.

I closed the diary, wiping away my tears.

I had presumed that Felice's antagonism towards Jenna was because the girl was with him on his last climb. But Dick's account had awakened in me a deeper insight. I realised that both of them blamed themselves for an accident which was beyond their control. Felice could not forgive herself that Con had died before there had been a reconciliation. Her anger had been motivated by her great love for him and fears for his safety.

And Jenna blamed herself for her foolish adventurous spirit, challenging Coniston Strong on his own ground. I understood at last, why Felice didn't want to talk about Con's death. The scar of the quarrel was still not healed. And poor Jenna, remembering so little, stoically bore what she believed to be her part in the accident. Perhaps a time would come when I could play the part of peacemaker.

CHAPTER TEN

Roger returned home late the following evening, and was already in the office when I arrived next day. He put his arms around me, and for the first time his kiss was long and passionate.

'Roger.' I extricated myself from his arms. 'What's up?'

He laughed, and I thought how attractive he was, and only a few short weeks ago I would have thrilled to his new passion.

'I had a good trip. Found an important picture, which will sell well.' He paused to allow me time to sit down. 'And,' he continued, 'as you know Jenna has at last agreed to give this clinic in Hungary a try. I've promised to take her and wait until the operation is over.'

'I hope with all my heart she will regain the use of her legs.' I paused, and then said consideringly, 'But don't you think she's being a bit premature about resigning from the partnership?' I'd forgotten until I spoke that Jenna had suggested I waited until Roger broke the news to me.

'I guessed she'd tell you. She will be well provided for, and her heart isn't in the Gallery, in fact she causes more trouble than she's worth. Father forced us both into the business. As it happens it suits me.' He smiled and reached for my hand. 'And what about you, Lindsay. Is your heart really in Reeds?'

I hesitated a moment. 'You know I love my work here, Roger. And in a way I feel a responsibility towards the Gallery, because of the arrangement your father made with Felice.'

'That's in no way binding on you. Felice's

pictures will always hang in this Gallery as long as it is open to the public.'

'I know that, Roger, and I'm sure she is appreciative.'

'I doubt it. She believes it to be her right. Father adored her.'

'Rubbish,' I said briskly. 'He was devoted to your mother.'

'Mother died a long time ago. Strange,' he said, 'that I should fall in love with Felice's daughter.'

I sat very still. My heart was thumping, and I felt the colour rising to my cheeks.

Roger didn't seem to notice. He was doodling on a used envelope. Suddenly he laid down his pencil and looked up. 'You know that Jenna's resignation leaves me free to offer a partnership to someone else. Will you consider it?'

'Do you think that's wise? I mean ...'

'You mean,' he said angrily, 'you don't want to be tied up here for ever. You want your freedom too. But don't you see, darling Lindsay, I want to marry you. You know I love you, we could be so happy together.' His face flushed and his eyes shone, and his direct glance compelled me to look at him. 'You don't have to decide now, I can wait.' He looked away, so that all I could see was the grim set of his jaw. 'Jenna says you went away for the weekend with Deauville. I can't allow that.' He jumped up and moving swiftly round

142

the desk hauled me to my feet, holding me desperately close.

I stiffened in his arms. 'I don't see it's any business of yours.'

'But it is. You are mine.'

'No, Roger. I am not. Please let me go.'

We had reached the point of no return; and I was angry. I wanted to go on working in the Gallery, I enjoyed the job. And I certainly would have accepted a partnership if it had been offered without strings.

He let go of me, and sat down heavily. There was the same sulky twist to his mouth that so often marred his sister's.

'I suppose Deauville hasn't told you his father passed him over. The family fortune is shared between his three brothers. I made it my business to find out. Odd, don't you think?'

'Not in the least. André Deauville wasn't Philippe's father.'

Roger looked at me in astonishment. 'He told you that? I didn't believe the Deauvilles when they hinted at something. Who is his father?'

'I've no idea.'

Roger sprang up and caught hold of my wrist. 'I don't believe you.'

'It's none of your business or mine. So let's forget it.'

He glowered at me, and then as so often happens he changed. He kissed my wrist before letting go, and smiled, his ill-temper forgotten.

143

'I'm sorry, darling Lindsay. I'm jealous, you know, silly of me. I don't have anything to be jealous of, do I?'

I ignored the question. 'Roger, I like working here very much. Can we stay on the old footing, at least until after Jenna's operation?'

He smiled. 'Of course, Lindsay. I can't run this damn Gallery without you.'

Which was a true statement.

The tension between us evaporated, and I breathed a sigh of relief. We settled down to business, and an in depth discussion of the recent sales which were rocketing. The ringing of the telephone interrupted, and I picked up the receiver, and announced the name of the Gallery. There was a second's silence, and then a voice asked for Roger. I recognised it even before I asked who was calling. I put my hand over the mouthpiece and whispered the word 'Ritter'. Roger stretched out a hand for the receiver, announcing his name. I watched his expression harden with some curiosity. There was a curt note in his voice when he spoke. 'We returned all your pictures, Mr Ritter. My sister gave you a receipt for ten, and ten were returned to you.'

He paused, listening. 'I don't know anything about a parcel. I'll make enquiries and call you back.' He banged down the receiver, and shouted for Davies.

He came, standing stolidly in the doorway.

'Come in, and shut the door,' Roger said impatiently. 'Ritter has just phoned, says he left a parcel with Jenna.'

Davies nodded. 'That's right. It has her name on the paper.'

'Please fetch it.'

Davies returned with the parcel which was obviously rolled canvases. A corner of the brown paper wrapping was torn, but a second layer concealed the contents.

'I suppose they are some more of Ritter's crumby canvases,' Roger grumbled.

Davies hesitated. 'Miss Jenna said I was on no account to show the contents to you. In fact, she was furious when I wouldn't promise. She told me to get out of the stockroom, and when she'd gone I went back but I couldn't see the parcel. It was only by chance I found it when I was moving some of those large frames.'

'How odd. I think we should open it, Roger.'

He shrugged his shoulders. 'I don't know what the hell Jenna is playing at, but if she thinks she can foist any of Ritter's pictures on me, she's sadly mistaken.' He paused, watching Davies unwrap the canvases, and unrolling them, laid them flat on the desk.

Roger drew in his breath sharply, and snatched his magnifying glass out of the desk drawer. Davies and I exchanged glances.

'Well, I'm damned,' he said. 'Look at these.'

Davies and I crowded round him.

'I don't believe it. I've never seen such good

copies,' I said.

'Not copies,' Roger traced the signature with butterfly touch. 'Originals.'

'But they can't be,' and then excitably I said, 'of course, I've seen them before in the Carvel Collection at the Thurley Manor Gallery, but I thought ...'

'These Constables and other pictures were stolen,' Davies said.

Roger's face was suffused with anger. 'How dare Ritter use Jenna. I'll—I'll—' he spluttered.

'Steady on, Mr Roger.' Davies straightened up. 'I think we must find out if Miss Jenna is involved.'

'Come off it, Davies. Jenna and stolen pictures,' his voice failed.

'She couldn't have known,' I faltered. 'He must have lied to her.'

'So Ritter is either a thief or a receiver of stolen goods,' Roger spoke distinctly. 'It looks like we've got him.'

'No, we haven't, Roger. He's been very clever. The police would never think of looking for stolen pictures in a reputable Gallery like ours. Hiding them here was a masterly stroke, especially involving Jenna.' My mind was logically cataloguing the consequences of the discovery of these pictures on our premises. 'We could be accused of receiving stolen goods.'

'And we will be ruined,' Roger said.

'Oh no we won't,' Davies said. 'We must get

rid of them.'

'Easier said than done. How?' I looked at Davies expectantly.

'Let me think.' Roger motioned him to a chair, and I sat down too; suddenly I felt weak and afraid. Roger was frowning. Only Davies appeared to be enjoying our dilemma. And I took heart, if anyone was capable of outwitting these villains Davies was. His long and honourable service in the Navy bore witness to his courage and ingenuity.

But now my fears were for Jenna. The police sergeant who had called to check our security arrangements had looked very grim when he'd mentioned the gang of picture thieves operating in this area. And Jenna was vulnerable, whether she was involved or not.

'I think we should get Jenna away to Hungary as soon as possible. She may be in some danger,' I said.

'That's very likely,' Davies agreed. 'I don't think we should make a move until you and Miss Jenna are out of the way, Mr Roger.'

'I won't clear off and leave you two. Suppose we just return the parcel to Ritter?'

Davies shook his head. 'Risky. If he gets caught I don't doubt he will make a statement that she was part of the plot.'

'He couldn't,' I protested.

'Oh yes he could,' Roger said heavily.

'So what do we do?' I was beginning to feel really frightened. 'What I don't understand,' I continued, 'is why Ritter has involved Jenna and the Gallery.'

'I think I can answer that,' Davies said. 'He's putting about a story that the Reeds are out to wreck his career as an artist. His desire for revenge goes back a long way. Both you and your father consistently refused to exhibit his work, Mr Roger. And the other reason is Miss Jenna rejected him.'

'What do you mean?' Roger scowled.

'He asked her to change her mind about marrying him. I didn't mean to eavesdrop, but they were in the stockroom and didn't see me. She told him to get lost, quite pithily, I thought.'

'He doesn't strike me as the kind of man who'd want to marry—' Roger paused, and added lamely, 'oh well, a girl with Jenna's problems.'

Davies said, 'He wants to marry a Reed. As Miss Jenna's husband he may think he can gain control of the Gallery through her.'

I looked helplessly from one to the other. 'What can we do?'

Davies smiled, a smile that boded ill for Ritter. 'How about this for a plan? We substitute two pictures in place of the ones in Ritter's parcel, and in the meantime we return the Constables to Thurley Gallery.'

'But,' I objected, 'when Ritter opens the parcel and finds the Constables gone, he'll think Jenna has double-crossed him, and come here breathing fire. And how are we going to return the pictures to Thurley without being caught?'

Davies outlined his plan. He would borrow a plain delivery van owned by a pal of his who owed him a favour. The parcel could then be delivered to the front door of Thurley House. It was a simple plan. The owners would be delighted to get back two of the most famous pictures in their collection, and the van and driver, Davies assured us, would never be traced.

It was a risk. I thought the scheme hare-brained, and said so.

'There isn't any other way,' Roger said. 'I won't forget your part in this, Davies,' he added.

The plans were formulated, and the time schedule agreed. As soon as Roger and Jenna were safely on the plane to Hungary, and Roger took some persuading that he had to go, I would notify Ritter we'd located his parcel, now containing the substitute canvases, but not until the Constables had been returned to Thurley. Here, at least, fortune smiled on us. Discreet enquiries elicited the fact that the Thurleys were abroad, and any parcel delivered to the Gallery would be placed in the safe awaiting their return. This meant the news wouldn't break for some time, and in the meantime the police might pick up Ritter and the gang.

Still, I was scared, and had good reason to be.

'All's well,' Davies said on his return from depositing Roger and Jenna at Manchester Airport, and assuring me the pictures had been safely returned, and no questions asked. But I can't say any of my fears were alleviated.

Telephoning Ritter was an ordeal. He was furious when I told him he couldn't speak to Jenna: she and Roger were away on holiday. 'Touring,' I said. 'No address.'

He called for his pictures which Davies handed over to him. And that I hoped was the end of the matter. But in my heart I knew it wasn't.

*　　*　　*

I would have liked to confide in Philippe, but we'd agreed that the matter should remain secret between the three of us. Philippe was waiting in the usual place outside the Gallery. It was six o'clock; and the kind of evening which must have encouraged Wordsworth to write poetry. I loved this place; I wanted no other.

We chose a pub in Troutbeck for our meal, and afterwards Philippe drove slowly along the narrow roads, savouring the ever changing scenery. At last he parked, and we alighted, and strolled up the gently rising moorland to a vantage point where the range of mountains

150

and lake were set before us.

'I wish I hadn't to go up to London,' Philippe said, 'but I'll be back at the weekend.' He paused, 'Lindsay, do you think I should give up the search for my father?'

'Can you give it up? Won't it always be there, nagging away in your mind?'

'Exactly. André Deauville gave me his name officially. I guess that was part of the bargain with my mother, but he cheated her in the end. He didn't change his Will until after her death.'

'Why then?'

'My brothers discovered André Deauville wasn't my father. They forced his hand. I don't blame them or him.'

He found a place for us to sit down, and put an arm round me.

'Can you forgive my obsession, Lindsay? If you say the word, I'll give up the search.'

I shook my head, and his arm tightened round me. 'Give me a little while longer,' he said.

I lifted my face to his and he kissed me hard and hungrily.

'I guess you must go on, Philippe. I do understand, really. Now that Dick has told me the truth about Con's death, everything seems different.' I repeated most of the words Dick had written, and he listened closely.

'If only I could talk to Felice about my father's death, I'm sure it would help her, but she shuts me up immediately.'

151

Philippe drove me home. I sensed his withdrawal; and his frustration was as nagging as mine had been. He had to know the truth, and I believed his only hope was Felice.

She was lying on the settee, and she waved a hand wearily as I sat down. 'Have you been out with that Frenchman?' she asked pettishly. Her blue gaze was hard and disturbing.

'Felice, why won't you admit you knew his mother? Her maiden name was Eve Cornell. Philippe was born before she married André Deauville. She told William Cornell you gave her three pictures. Philippe has two, and William the other. A springtime picture, except for the empty boat on the lake. I think,' I said carefully, 'you know the name of Eve's lover.'

A wild look crossed her face, and she sprang up from the settee. 'If you don't stop pestering me with these ridiculous stories, I shall ask you to go away. I will not be questioned.' There was a sob in her voice. 'I tell you it wasn't my fault.'

'What wasn't your fault?'

'Nothing. I didn't mean that. You are trying to confuse me. Go away and leave me alone.' She flung out of the room and I heard her footsteps hammering on the polished boards of the stairs. Her door shut with a final bang that told me plainly that maybe the time was coming when we might have to part company.

And yet how could I abandon her? A surge of love for her overwhelmed me; I longed to comfort her, and found her rejection hard to bear.

Barney climbed on to the window seat beside me. He laid his head on my knee. His soulful steady gaze indicated he knew I wouldn't fail to take him for a walk. There was just enough light left in the sky to guide us a short way on the fells. Returning, Dora was waiting at her gate. 'Felice has been yelling for you.'

'What does she want?'

'To show you her new painting. She's in the studio.'

The cottage was quiet, the studio door shut. I opened the door quietly and walked in.

'Oh there you are, darling. Come and look at this.'

I caught my breath as I gazed at the peaceful scene. No High Sail, or empty boat, just a sense of a golden afternoon; so serene, no tremor on the lake, the long line of fells darkly green, and a clear blue sky with not a cloud on the horizon.

'All's well,' she said, and kissed me.

But of course it wasn't.

CHAPTER ELEVEN

It was now the height of the tourist season. The Gallery, and the adjacent gift and bookshops were thronged with customers all day. There had been a feature on Felice in the local paper,

153

and this had stirred up intense interest in her pictures. Davies and I were kept busy all that Saturday, and I was looking forward to Roger's return from Hungary.

Towards the end of the day Davies brought me a strong pot of tea, and I suggested he sat down and joined me.

'We've no more of "Her" pictures in the stockroom,' he announced. I smiled, his reference to my mother as 'Her' always gave me a warm feeling. 'That chap from the London gallery is coming on Monday, and he'll be looking for a fair selection.'

'I'll tackle Felice tonight. She's been working very hard, and I'm sure has quite a few canvases ready. I'll bring them round to the Gallery tomorrow, so we can hang them first thing on Monday.'

Davies stirred his tea reflectively. 'Ritter was here.'

I started. 'Did he speak to you? What did he want?'

'He asked me for Miss Jenna's address. When I denied knowing it, he was most aggressive, uttering all kinds of threats.'

'Like what?' I asked apprehensively.

'He said he hoped we had a good insurance policy. It would be sad if the Gallery caught fire.'

I felt a cold shiver down my back.

'I told him if there was any vandalism we'd know where to send the police.'

'Davies, I don't like it. I wish Roger was back.'

'Don't worry, Miss Lindsay. I intend watching that one.'

'Well, just be careful, Davies. I couldn't bear anything happening to you.'

Just on closing-time Dick Outhwaite walked in. He took my hand and kissed my cheek. I felt I was forgiven. 'Felice has asked Peggy and me to supper, but I wanted a word with you first,' he said.

'Dick, I'm sorry if I forced you into revealing the circumstances of Con's death. But I had to know.'

He smiled, and squeezed my hand before letting go. 'I'm glad you do. I would have spoken about it long ago, but Felice was adamant I shouldn't. Have you mentioned it to her?'

'Of course not. Will you take your diary, I locked it up in the safe here.' I unlocked the safe and handed it to him. 'Dick, why were you so reluctant to talk to me about Con?'

'I don't really know, except Felice made us promise. And we have always protected her ever since the first day she came to our house. Con asked me many years ago, to look after her if he died first.'

Dick's protection was obvious when at last, bone weary, I parked my car outside our cottage and joined our guests. I gratefully accepted a drink which Dick poured for me, and Dora insisted I ate the supper she'd left for me in the dining-room. I was almost too drained to eat, but made a valiant attempt under Dora's watchful eye. When she went to the kitchen to make coffee, Dick appeared.

'Do you mind if I sit here with you?'

I motioned him to the carver at the end of the table, and he sat down, crossing his legs and leaning back.

'What's on your mind Dick?'

'Roger has informed me Jenna wishes to retire from the Gallery. As you know I'm one of the trustees of the Reed estate. Roger suggests you as the new partner. I have consulted the other trustees and this will be quite acceptable to them.'

'But not to me,' I said crisply.

Dick looked up. Deep blue eyes beneath bushy brows, screwed up in surprise.

'I understood Roger has spoken to you.'

'He has. But there are strings.'

'I don't know of any.'

'Marriage.'

'I don't understand. I always thought you and Roger ...'

I shook my head.

'Is there another man?'

Dumbly I nodded.

'Is it Deauville?'

'Yes, but ...'

'I know. Felice doesn't like him. Peggy and I thought him charming.' He hesitated a
156

moment. 'He puts me in mind of someone—' he sighed, 'imagination, I guess.'

'Just a minute, Dick. André Deauville wasn't Philippe's father.'

'Is that so.'

I reflected that Dick's training as a lawyer precluded him from being astonished at any of the turns and twists which rule our fate.

'Philippe won't ask me or any other woman to marry him until he knows his antecedents. He has this obsessional fear of bad blood—or something like that. Dick, when you first met Felice, she was friendly with a girl called Eve Cornell. Eve was Philippe's mother. Do you remember her?'

This time I'd got beneath his skin. His cheeks blanched, and his eyes narrowed to glinting slits. I leaned forward. 'You did know her,' I accused. 'Is that why Philippe reminds you of someone? Felice pretends she didn't know her. Why?'

'I can't speak for Felice,' he said harshly.

'You must. Don't you see my happiness is at stake. I love Philippe,' I said softly.

For a long moment he stared at me. His indecision was painful to watch, but I had to press on. I was filled with a rising excitement, and an expectancy beyond all reason.

'Why won't you or Felice speak about Eve Cornell? Didn't you know she went to France from here and married André Deauville?'

'Of course I didn't know.' He stood up.

'Dick, please wait. Why can't you talk about her?'

'Not now. Peggy will be wondering where I am,' he said and hurried from the room.

I was too tired to think. I rose unsteadily, and mounted the stairs clinging to the banisters. In my room I opened wide the window, and fully dressed flung myself down on the bed and wept.

*   *   *

I woke early, the cottage was quiet. For a moment I couldn't think why I was lying on the bed with all my clothes on; then I remembered my conversation with Dick, and its unsatisfactory conclusion.

Wearily I shed my clothes, and ran a bath. I soaked in the hot scented water, still feeling utterly bewildered by Dick's behaviour. Was he again protecting Felice? If so, from what?

I dried myself and scrambled into jeans and a sweater and crept downstairs. In the kitchen Barney greeted me rapturously. I made a pot of tea, aware of the hope in the dog's eyes.

'OK.' I gave in as always. 'Come on.'

He restrained his excitement until we were outside. Then he whisked off, lost momentarily among Con's Christmas trees. We had the fell to ourselves—except for the sheep—and I was renewed by the peace and quiet. We took a different route back which brought us down to

158

the lake. At the inlet opposite the Outhwaites' house I concealed myself from any watching eyes.

All the little pieces of the mystery were jigging about in my mind, but I couldn't make sense of them. Barney plunged into the lake; he loved water. I let him swim for a while, and then called him back. He hurtled along the bank and shook himself vigorously showering ice cold drops over me.

The sun had risen above the tip of the fells, and the whole landscape was bathed in magical first light which Felice depicted with such feeling and artistry. She was sitting at the breakfast table when we arrived back at the cottage. She enjoyed the Sunday newspapers, dropping the sheets around her as she skimmed through them.

'Good morning, darling.' She was as bright as the day. 'Are you rested? I looked in on you last night, and you were dead to the world.'

I kissed her soft cheek, and unexpectedly she put up her arms and pulled me close. 'I need you, Lindsay,' she murmured. 'Don't leave me.'

'I'm not going anywhere.' I sat down and poured coffee.

'No, I mustn't say that. Con used to get angry when I begged him never to leave me.'

I looked at her curiously. 'Surely that was the last thought in his head.'

'I hope so,' she said. Suddenly brisk she

159

asked, 'Shall I scramble eggs?'

I buttered toast. 'I took Barney to the lake. He had a swim. It's quite shallow at that inlet opposite the Outhwaites' house.'

'Really,' she drawled. 'I never walk to the lake now.' She stood up, scattering sheets of newspaper. 'Dora and I are going to church.'

I gathered together the sheets of newspapers and glanced at the headlines, waiting for her to return. She'd changed and looked very smart in a white suit with navy accessories. 'Darling, I thought the three of us could lunch at the Lake End Hotel. Will you meet us there?'

'Count me out. I've some work to do.'

'I hope Roger appreciates your devotion to duty. He's a lucky man.' She came close; and her familiar perfume overwhelmed. She bent and kissed my cheek. 'Roger asked me if I'd mind if you and he married ...'

'Hang on. I've no intention of marrying Roger.'

She frowned and drew on her gloves. 'I shall pray you come to your senses.' She departed, calling imperiously to Dora.

Had she always been the great manipulator? Had Con let her dictate? Was that the deep reason I'd dragged up my roots and preferred an independent life away from her—and Con?

Towards lunch-time I made some sandwiches, and Barney and I walked back to the inlet of the lake. I seemed to be drawn by some mysterious thread, tantalising in its

160

obscurity.

From this vantage point, I observed a rowing boat anchored in the centre of the lake. The two men in it were fishing, and sat motionless. And then one reeled in his line; I saw the flash of silver as he unhooked the fish. The other man appeared to protest; waving his hand, and unexpectedly he stood up. The boat rocked dangerously, and shipped water. In the quiet I heard the other bloke shout, 'You fool, sit down.' He shifted his oars in the lock, and started to row away. I realised with a start how easily a boat can capsize.

An empty boat. In the middle of a familiar lake. Teasing on the edge of my mind was some last piece which would solve the mystery of Felice's obsession with this place.

Leisurely we walked back, and as I opened the cottage door I heard the insistent ring of the telephone, and lifting the receiver, my heart leapt as Philippe's familiar tones reached me.

'Hallo love. I'm on my way home. Will you meet me at the Lake End Hotel for a spot of dinner?'

'I'd like that.'

'Great. Make it eight o'clock. Look after yourself, Lindsay, my dear.' There was a different note in his voice, as if he had come to some momentous decision, and like a fool, I was filled with hope.

* * *

'More pictures?' Felice questioned some time later. 'I suppose there are a few in the studio. Have a look, but don't take any without asking me.'

I rarely went to the studio alone. Although Felice didn't display a keep out notice, for me, there was always this indefinable feeling of trespassing on sacred ground. The smell of paint and turpentine; the harsh light, unshaded; the carved mahogany chair with a scarlet cloth flung across the arms, were all part of a world to which I didn't feel entitled to enter.

There was a stack of canvases already framed propped up against one wall. Glancing at them I remembered they'd been returned from The Walker Gallery in Manchester, where an exhibition of Lakeland artists had been held. These, obviously, Felice wouldn't have any compunction in putting up for sale. There was a smaller stack of canvases, some unfinished, and one or two which lacked the spark which set Felice's work apart. I was amazed at how prolific she was, and turned at last to a smaller framed stack away from the others.

Felice wasn't a keen portrait painter, but these I judged to be good. The topmost was an excellent likeness of Dora. Her joyous spirit seemed to spring out of the canvas, self-evident in the half smile, the glint of happiness in her eyes. I gazed on familiar faces; Dick, Peggy, Roger and Con. At the bottom of the pile, wrapped in a cloth, was another picture. I uncovered it and gasped in surprise. Surely Felice hadn't painted Philippe? I moved under the northern window where the light beat down on the canvas, and realised my mistake. This wasn't a portrait of Philippe, but some man he vaguely resembled; perhaps my initial mistake was my first glimpse encompassing only the happy curve of the mouth, the brightness of the eyes, the tilt of the head. It struck me there might be a family resemblance, seen in the half smile lingering round the mouth, the shape of cheek and chin; the sparkle in the eyes.

Could this faint likeness be coincidental? I wrapped it up and carried it into the sitting-room. Felice was watching television. I switched off, and uncovering the canvas held it up before her.

'Who is this?' I spoke more sharply than I intended.

She narrowed her eyes, and screwed up her mouth, her voice was harsh. 'Where did you find that? I thought ...'

'You'd hidden it. Why?'

She looked at me. Her face was flushed. 'I asked Con to destroy it.'

'Why?'

'I don't want to be reminded, ever. Con said I wouldn't always feel guilty.'

'Guilty? What on earth are you talking about?'

'The accident. We were in the boat ...' She hid her face in her hands. And involuntarily I recalled the scene I'd witnessed earlier in the day. The two fishermen in the boat, the near capsize.

'Hadn't you better tell me about it?' I said gently.

She sighed, and uncovered her face. 'I suppose so. If I don't, sooner or later, Philippe Deauville will dig out the truth. Give it to me.'

She held out her hands for the portrait, and gazed steadily at it for a full minute. Then sighing once again, she set it aside. 'I don't need this to remind me of him,' she said quietly. 'You don't forget how a man you loved, smiled, spoke; his little mannerisms, the way he held you in his arms.'

'You loved this man. Before Con?'

She nodded. 'Before Con—but not after, you must believe that.'

'Who is he?'

'Leslie Outhwaite,' she said.

'But, I don't understand. There is a likeness to Philippe.'

She nodded again. 'Why not? Philippe is Leslie's son.'

I started at her aghast.

She stood up. 'I don't want to talk about it.'

'I do. Sit down, mother.'

She sank back into her chair.

'It will help you to tell me the truth. Con always said hidden fears fester. Don't you see, by telling me you'll exorcise these guilty feelings.'

'Perhaps, Lindsay. I don't know, darling, I don't know.'

I prompted her gently.

'You met Leslie at art college, didn't you?'

'Yes. He was an exceptional artist, and he encouraged me. He brought me here to stay with Dick and Peggy. And I knew that this scenery was all I really wanted to paint. I fell in love with the man and the landscape. It was peculiar—like a reincarnation. I knew the shapes and colours of these mountains in my bones. Leslie was the same. The few pictures of the mountains he painted were mysterious; so vital, they defied time. Dick and Peggy can't bear to look at them now, so they have locked them away.'

'And did Leslie love you?'

'At first, yes. And then Eve Cornell came.' Felice closed her eyes, arms tightly round breasts, rocking herself like a child. 'I didn't know, you see, they were secretly lovers. He told me, that day in the boat.'

'The boat,' I repeated. 'The empty boat?'

She nodded. 'He told me Eve was carrying their child. He was going to marry her. I jumped up filled with an almighty rage. The boat capsized and threw us both in the water. I swam to the shore, but Leslie drowned.'

165

I put my arms round her; holding her shivering body close.

'I never admitted it was my fault. I hated Eve, she took him from me.'

'It was an accident, Felice. No one was to blame.'

'Not true. I blamed Leslie in my heart; I thought he'd cheated me.'

She sighed, and tears ran down her cheeks. I wiped them away. At this moment I loved her with all my heart.

'Do you hate Philippe because he is Leslie's son?'

'No. Because he is Eve's. Will you tell him?'

'Yes,' I said. 'Yes, I'll tell him.'

*　　*　　*

Felice approved my choice of pictures to take to the Gallery. At least, approval wasn't quite the right word. Holding up the canvases before her, she said 'Take what you like. It doesn't matter any more.'

It would matter to her again, and I took care only to choose the ones which hadn't any hidden meaning for her. It would take her a long time to come to terms with Leslie's and Con's deaths, but perhaps by confessing to me the healing process had already started.

The tiny pieces of the jigsaw which had for so long puzzled me were beginning to fall into place. Because of Eve's perfidy, she had

166

suspected Jenna of conspiring to wrench Coniston from her.

I pondered over Felice's revelations as I dressed for my dinner with Philippe. I imagined his excitement and joy when he knew he did belong here, and his instinct had been right. I had a feeling the evening would be momentous, and with this thought in mind, I took out of the wardrobe a new dress I'd been saving for an occasion. Blue is my colour, and complements the shade of my eyes, and the shining smooth hair I had allowed to grow. The mirror reflected something else: the gleam of hope in my eyes.

I called to Felice, and she helped me stack the framed pictures and rolled canvases into the boot of the car.

'Are you meeting Philippe?' she asked with trepidation.

'Dinner at the Lake End Hotel after I've taken these to the Gallery.'

'I'm afraid ...' she began.

'Don't be,' I said firmly.

I drove into town, and steered the car down the narrow alley at the back of the Gallery, parking opposite the door which opens up into the stockroom, and squeezed out between the car and the wall. It took me a moment or two to find the right keys, and I opened the door, prepared to switch off the burglar alarm at the first bleep. Only it didn't make a sound. Puzzled, I switched on the stockroom light.

167

The alarm was in the 'Off' position. Surely Davies hadn't forgotten to set it? Then I remembered I'd told him I was bringing in some of Felice's pictures, so perhaps he was already in the Gallery?

I unloaded the pictures, and locked up the car and the outside door and went through into the office. The glass door into the Gallery was open. There were no lights on, but little patches of pale evening sunshine filtered through the high windows and patterned the floor. The silence was uncanny.

Suddenly I was aware of quiet footsteps. Darting to the door I saw a figure at the far end of the Gallery. 'Davies,' I shouted. 'What are you doing here? You gave me a hell of a fright.'

He didn't answer. The figure loomed nearer, and was momentarily illuminated in a patch of sunlight. I drew a gasping breath, no face, a stocking mask, and the gleam of a knife in one hand.

CHAPTER TWELVE

I froze. Heart hammering, hands clenched. A second figure appeared, and a third.

The character with the knife motioned me back into the office. I tried to move, but my legs buckled and I would have sunk to the floor if one of the others hadn't caught hold of me and propelled me to a chair.

I couldn't believe this was happening to me, and I felt a hysterical desire to scream. The third figure approached. He was thickset, and wore a black polo-necked sweater. As my gaze travelled upwards, he peeled off his mask, and I was staring into the pebble dark eyes of John Ritter.

'You,' I gasped.

'Who else? Did you think I'd let you get away with stealing my pictures.'

'I don't understand. We returned your pictures ...'

'But not the Constables. I want them. Now.'

He moved closer, bending over me. His breath stank of whisky and I pressed back into the chair.

'Where are they?'

'Not here,' I mumbled.

'Lying won't do you any good. Tear the place apart,' he yelled to his two henchmen. He retreated to the doorway where he could keep an eye on the searchers and on me. When they didn't find the pictures, and they wouldn't, what would they do?

It seemed like a lifetime listening to the destructive noises coming from the Gallery. My gaze never wavered from Ritter.

At last defeat was admitted.

Ritter stood over me, the knife in his hand.

'Where are they hidden?' His request softly spoken, nevertheless was vibrant with menace.

I plucked up the remnants of my courage. 'Back where they belong.'

His disbelieving look might have made me smile in other circumstances.

'I don't get it. The police ... ?'

'No, Mr Ritter. Not the police. The Constables have been returned to Thurley Grange Gallery anonymously.'

'Surely Reed wouldn't be such a fool as to walk in the Gallery with the pictures under his arm. "Here you are, Sir. I found them under a gooseberry bush."'

'Of course not,' I snapped.

'Then how?'

'Let's say they were successfully returned. By the front door.'

'You're lying.'

'No. Just fighting back against thieves and receivers like you.'

He closed in on me. The knife was poised above my heart.

'One more crack like that, Miss Lindsay Strong, and your beauty will be spoilt for life.' Our glances met. I would not lower my gaze.

After a second he stepped back. 'I've no quarrel with you,' he mumbled. 'Only the Reeds. So Jenna double-crossed me.'

'She didn't know anything about it.'

'She sure did. We are partners.'

'A likely story. Jenna would never jeopardise the good name of her brother or the Gallery. You used her—cruelly. But at least she had the sense to reject your offer of marriage,' I said with great satisfaction.

His face suffused with anger. 'Not quite. You see I hold the ace. Sooner or later she'd have agreed to marry me, because if she's as loyal as you say, she wouldn't want stolen pictures to be found here.'

'Blackmail won't get you anywhere. Jenna has resigned. She has nothing to do with it now.'

The knife quivered in his hand. 'You're a damn good liar.'

'Go away, Ritter,' I said. 'I've told you where the Constables are.'

'I don't believe you, but I'll soon find out.' He leaned across the desk, and drew the telephone towards him. He asked the operator for the number of Thurley House, and when he was connected he spoke in a soft slurred voice. 'Good evening,' he said. 'I'm from the *Daily News*. I understand two of the pictures stolen from your private gallery, have been returned. Can you confirm it.'

I prayed that the Thurleys had come home and that the parcel had been opened. I couldn't hear the voice at the other end, but Ritter's expression said it all. I sighed with relief. He slammed down the receiver, and his anger was like a live animal consuming him.

He yelled to his accomplices, 'Tie her up.'

They used picture cord, and yanked it so viciously round my wrists and ankles it seared

171

into the flesh.

'No use screaming,' he said. 'And believe me, if you call the police it's curtains for Reed.'

The office light was snapped off, and I heard their retreating footsteps. In a moment all noise ceased. I began to cry, silently.

*   *   *

Time was of no consequence. I was beyond time, suspended in a vacuum of pain and despair. Gingerly I tried to move to ease the cords, but there was no give in them. And suddenly I thought of my father. I thought of the day when we'd gone climbing in the Langdales, and the mist had dropped as swiftly as birds of prey swooped down.

'We stay put, lassie,' he'd said. 'It's always possible to ride out any emergency. Never panic, lassie, never panic.' He seemed close in that instant. His voice was in my head, his love in my heart.

I breathed deeply, and reviewed the situation. At worst, I might have to endure the night until Davies opened up in the morning, but at best Philippe might telephone Felice when I didn't turn up for our date.

I closed my eyes and willed Philippe to care enough to look for me. My longing for him at that moment was so great, that I almost forgot the agonising pain in my wrists and ankles.

'Don't panic,' I said aloud. 'Don't panic.'

After a little while I think I drifted into unconsciousness. When I came to, the light from the windows was a pale cold blue. And suddenly I couldn't bear it any longer. I screamed, and screamed. And above the noise of my own voice I became aware of a thudding and banging. Abruptly I stopped as the sound of splintering wood sent my heart racing. I listened to heavy footsteps on the wooden floor in the stockroom, and then a familiar voice was calling my name.

He burst into the office. Behind him was the burly figure of Sergeant Brack.

'Philippe,' I whispered.

'It's all right, darling.'

Carefully he cut the cords with the Sergeant's knife, and gently rubbed my wrists and ankles to restore the circulation. Tears ran down my cheeks, but I wasn't sure if it was relief or the agony of the circulating blood to my limbs.

The Sergeant and the two police constables accompanying him began a systematic search of the Gallery, and it didn't take them long to find Davies in the Gents toilet.

'Bound and gagged,' the Sergeant said, supporting Davies and lowering him into a chair.

He was ashen-faced, his eyes black with anger.

'What happened?' I asked weakly.

'Kidnapped. In my own house, too. Forced

me here with the keys. They didn't expect you.'

I struggled out of the safety of Philippe's arms, and took hold of Davies's hands. 'Are you hurt?'

'No bones broken. Plenty of bruises. They didn't take me easily.' The old familiar grin creased his face.

Sergeant Brack said, 'I warned you there was a gang of picture thieves operating in this district. Probably the same gang did over Thurley Grange Gallery. Well, I'll get the fingerprint blokes in, and you'd better check on your stock.'

'They wore gloves,' Davies said.

'I don't suppose you recognised any of them? Three, you say.'

Davies shook his head. 'They wore stocking masks.'

'What about you, Miss Strong?'

'I think,' I said, and even as I spoke I couldn't betray Ritter. Because of Jenna. Because I didn't know how foolish she had been. I closed my eyes, the faces were whirling, the voices became faint, and all I knew was that Philippe's arms were holding me safe.

*   *   *

Felice sat with me all that night. Every time I opened my eyes she was there, wrapped in a rug close to the bedside. And when I stretched out my hand she gripped it tightly.

174

Philippe had driven Davies and me to the hospital for a quick check-up. We refused to stay in, and Philippe brought us both back to the cottage, and insisted on staying. Felice was grateful. Dora took charge, and beds were made up for the two men.

My main anxiety was Roger. Sergeant Brack had telephoned him, and I was sure Roger would be worried sick. I would have liked to speak to him, but couldn't face his questioning. Next morning, Philippe and Davies tried to persuade me to stay away from the Gallery, but I insisted on accompanying them. Davies seemed little the worse for his experience. His bruised face would take time to heal, but his fury at being duped injected him with a fierce energy and a thirst for revenge.

A police guard had been left on the shattered door overnight, and when the three of us arrived at the Gallery, Sergeant Brack was already there. He informed us that Roger was flying back today, and he'd phone from the airport. 'Mr Reed was very co-operative. He gave us a name. But when we arrived at the house, the bird had flown. Don't worry, we'll get him and the rest of the gang.'

The Gallery looked as if a maniac had been at work. 'You knew it was Ritter,' Davies accused, as we began the heartbreaking task of clearing up. 'Why didn't you speak up?'

'I couldn't,' I said. 'I wasn't sure how deeply Jenna was involved.

175

'Yes,' he said and smiled. 'I would have done the same.'

Felice's pictures seemed to have been the main target for the vandalism. Davies's expression grew grimmer, as each new outrage was revealed.

'I'll never forgive Ritter for this,' he said holding up one of the ruined canvases. 'The sooner he's behind bars the better.'

We set to work and Davies and I were glad of Philippe's help. We kept the Gallery closed, but had to open the shops which were busy and staff couldn't be spared to help us.

Roger arrived at lunch-time. He came storming down the Gallery and grabbed me tightly in his arms. 'Oh God,' he murmured, 'I'd never have forgiven myself if anything had happened to you.'

'I'm fine.' I extricated myself from his arms.

'I should have been here.'

'Lucky you weren't. Ritter was breathing vengeance on you and Jenna. He says she double-crossed him.'

Roger scowled, and headed for the office, sweeping me along with him. He shouted for Davies before opening the cupboard where he kept a bottle of whisky and glasses.

Roger's scowl deepened at the sight of Davies's bruised face. He pushed a chair forward and put a glass in his hand.

'What happened?' he asked, taking his seat at the other side of the desk. Davies drank his whisky and set down the glass. His face seemed to have aged overnight. He repeated his story up to the point where the police had found him. His slightly apologetic tone brought a quick response from Roger.

'You did well, man. There wasn't any way you could have fought three of them off alone.'

Roger turned to me. I took up the story where I'd opened the rear door, ready to switch off the burglar alarm.

Roger questioned me closely. 'Were you surprised to find the alarm not set?'

'Not really. I had mentioned to Davies I'd bring some more of Felice's pictures in on Sunday, and I presumed Davies had come in earlier and switched off the alarm. I carried the pictures in, and the next moment ...' I shivered, remembering the horror of that moment when the masked figure had loomed up before me. And with a quaking heart I recalled the threats Ritter had made against Roger and Jenna.

'Roger, I think you should warn the clinic in Hungary to keep a close watch on Jenna until Ritter is caught. Does she know?'

Roger gave a heartrending sigh. 'I had to tell her. I had to know if she was involved with Ritter. The little fool admitted she knew he was up to something, but she didn't know what, or that he was prepared to drag her into it. I've told the Sergeant that Ritter might try and attack Jenna, and he has informed the local

177

police. I can't forgive her for getting mixed up with that villain.'

Davies said, 'I don't think she meant any harm.'

'You're right, Davies. At first it was just a lark, a sop to the boredom, and then she became frightened, and Ritter threatened her.'

'When the police catch Ritter, will he implicate Jenna?'

'I think not. He's got no proof of her involvement. I've seen to that.'

I sighed with relief, and suddenly tears filled my eyes.

Roger hauled me to my feet. 'You're all in, Lindsay. Home for you, and try to rest.' He escorted me down the Gallery to where Philippe was waiting. Philippe took my arm.

'Look after her,' Roger said, and turning, went back to the office without glancing round.

I had a strange feeling that something important had ended; I wasn't sure if the future would open out, or close round my head.

*　　　*　　　*

Felice was ensconced in the sitting-room. She lay on the settee, a lavender impregnated pad over her eyes. She sat up as we entered. 'Oh there you are, darling.'

'Aren't you well?' I couldn't allay my anxiety for her.

'Just resting.' She rolled her feet off the

settee, and standing saw Philippe. Expression revealed the swift procession of her thoughts. 'Do come in, Philippe,' she said. 'I expect you'd like something to eat.'

'I'll get it,' I said.

'Certainly not, darling. Dora has left food all ready on the dining-room table. I'll just go and make the coffee.'

She fluttered away to the kitchen. I made to follow her, but Philippe caught hold of my arm. 'Sit down, I'll go.'

I didn't want to be left alone with my thoughts. They tangled one against the other, totally incoherent. And this frightened me more than I can say. I sat down, kicked off my shoes, and leaning back, tried to relax. I knew I could make sense, understand my feelings, if I could only find the strand which would guide me safely through the maze. As if I was physically in a maze, I felt enclosed by high hedges; thick with growing menace.

Barney came snuffling in from the garden. He put his front paws up on my knees and licked my face. And instantly, I was at peace. His expressive eyes, so full of steadfast loyalty, renewed my courage.

Philippe called me into the dining-room. Dear kind Dora had taken so much trouble with the food. It was her way of expressing sympathy. Felice sat down at the head of the table, and Philippe and I on either side. We helped ourselves to the cold meat and salads.

Felice was nervous; she flapped and fluttered like a bird with a broken wing. If Philippe noticed, he didn't make any remark, but she was making me feel I couldn't sit there much longer.

She wasn't really listening when I told her Roger had flown home, and that so far the police hadn't caught up with the thieves.

'I've been thinking Lindsay. You must go away, a holiday. Why don't we go to Italy?'

'I can't run away, now. I wouldn't dream of leaving Roger.'

'Run away?' She gave me a penetrating look. 'What are you saying? A holiday isn't running away. You're had a terrible experience, and it will tell on your nerves. I'm sure Roger would agree with me.'

'I'm sorry, Mother, but I can't possibly go away.'

'You'll have a nervous breakdown,' Felice prophesied.

'Of course I won't,' I said sharply, and bent down to give Barney a titbit.

'I don't like that dog being fed at the table,' Felice said. 'Do stop it. He's slobbering all over you. Really Lindsay, you do need someone to look after you.'

And there we had it. She was staking her claim.

Philippe said, 'I'm sure Lindsay is well able to take care of herself.' He paused. 'There are other people who also might feel they can take care of her.'

'Who?' Felice asked sharply.

'Hey! Stop talking about me as if I wasn't here.'

'Darling, don't be silly. I want the best for you.'

'And so do I,' Philippe said.

Felice's smile was thin. 'I'm sure you do. And of course we mustn't forget Roger. He is so kind, and so fond of Lindsay, and he has a prior claim, I believe.' She cast a sidelong glance at Philippe. 'When does the new school term start?'

'In a week or two, but I'm not going back.'

'Why not?' Felice's glance was icy.

'I've resigned. I've been offered a position at Overbury School.'

My heart leapt with the kind of anguished hope that is so hard to bear.

'Will you take it?' I said. 'Overbury is only about ten miles from here.'

'Yes, I've accepted. It's a job I really want. I'm to teach French and cricket. I don't want to go far away. I feel so at home here. Ridiculous, of course. I was born in France.'

Why did he say that now, with such wistfulness? Felice was sitting very still. Her gaze was fixed on the view through the open window; the rounded shoulder of the fell, and the high peaks beyond.

Abruptly she stood up. 'Come, both of you. I've something to show Philippe.'

She led the way into the studio. Her easel was covered with a cloth, and she whipped it off, and turned the canvas to the light. Philippe stepped politely forward, and then stopped dead.

'Who is that?' He caught hold of her arm.

'Leslie Outhwaite. I painted that portrait thirty years ago, just before he was drowned in the lake.'

'He—we—' Philippe stammered. His face was flushed.

'You see the likeness?' Felice was composed. 'And why not? He was your mother's lover. Your father.'

'Are you sure?' He tightened his hold on her arm and she grimaced.

'Of course I'm sure. He told me he loved your mother, and she was carrying his child. He hoped to marry her.'

Only I knew what this telling must have cost her.

'But he didn't,' Philippe said.

'No. He died.'

'How did he die?' His voice was harsh.

She disengaged her arm. 'Lindsay will tell you.' She brushed close to me in the doorway and kissed me lightly.

'It's up to you,' she whispered. 'It's up to you.'

*   *   *

182

'She knew who I was the moment I crossed the doorstep. Didn't she?'

I nodded.

I turned the easel away from the light and covered it with the cloth. He didn't stop me, but stood there breathing heavily, as if all the air in the room was used up. I felt my throat constricting.

'Let's walk down to the lake,' I said. 'I feel stifled.'

He nodded, and taking my arm guided me out into the garden. The day was sultry; thunder clouds were banking over the fells, and yet in the west the sun still shone in defiance of the approaching storm.

'There's going to be a storm.'

'It will pass.'

Holding tightly on to my arm, he measured his steps to mine. I breathed deeply, needing the space of the fells and the sky. Space to fight the fear of enclosure; those claustrophobic moments when I'd been trussed up in the dark.

The lake was motionless, save for the tiny frill of waves breaking against the bank, its unreflecting inky depths taking a cue from the darkening sky. The inlet opposite the Outhwaites' house was deserted. We sat in the shadow of some rocks, there was the warm smell of earth thirsting for the coming rain. He put his arm around me, and drew me close.

'How did my father die?' Philippe asked, savouring the word.

'He was drowned. In this lake.'

'Tell me.'

I was caught in the net of deceit of my mother's making. I could lie, prevaricate. I could say a sudden storm blew up; or someone made an abrupt movement in the boat. Philippe might be satisfied. He was not so much concerned with the actual death of Leslie Outhwaite as the truth of Felice's statement that the man was his father. And even now I longed to protect Felice.

He has a right to know the truth, I thought, the same right I'd exercised in probing the truth of my father's death. I loved Philippe too deeply to deny him the right of knowledge.

'Felice and Leslie Outhwaite attended the same art college,' I began. 'That summer vacation he invited her to stay with him at the Outhwaites' home. She came, and fell in love with him, and with the landscape she's made so much her own. She thought Leslie loved her, her dreams were of him, and the certainty that they had a wonderful future before them. And so she agreed to marry him,' I paused and looked across the lake. 'Then Eve came with a party from Liverpool University. She made Felice's acquaintance, admiring her paintings, and Felice introduced her to Leslie. When Eve's party moved on, she stayed, and was invited to stay at the Outhwaites' home.'

'A threesome,' Philippe said reflectively.

'Yes. They were together all that summer.

184

Leslie became captivated by your mother. He and Eve fell violently in love. They kept it a secret from Felice, until the day she and Leslie were out in the boat, and he told her that Eve was expecting his child, and he asked Felice to release him from their engagement. Felice sprang up, and the boat capsized. Felice was a strong swimmer, but Leslie wasn't. She didn't know he had a heart complaint; the water was icy cold, and he had an attack and drowned.'

'An accident,' Philippe said in a firm voice.

'She's blamed herself all these years.'

'Poor, poor Felice.'

My heart turned over with love for him, his compassion was balm to my spirit.

'So now you know. The Outhwaites have been told.'

He stood up, and holding out his hands pulled me to my feet.

'It couldn't be better. I knew I belonged here from the first moment I looked at my mother's pictures. Well, my dearest Lindsay, is there any hope for me? I feel bad about Roger. Perhaps I shouldn't ask?'

'It depends.'

'On what?'

'Love.'

His arms slid round my shoulders drawing me close, and he kissed me. 'I love you with all my heart, Lindsay. I won't ever give you up.'

'I love you, Philippe. I was afraid ...'

'Nothing to fear now.' He kissed me long

and hard.

Lost in the ecstasy of our shared love we ignored the heavy drops of rain which were spotting the lake, and hissing on the dry earth. At last Philippe looked round for shelter.

'Shall we run for it?' he asked.

I was loath to leave this enchanted place and time, and Philippe sensing my mood took off his jacket and held it over our heads. From the Outhwaite jetty a boat sped across the lake.

Dick shouted as he throttled back and bumped gently against the bank. 'Come on! You'll get soaked.'

He held out his hand to steady me as I clambered aboard and sat down. Philippe followed. Dick took his hand in a firm grip.

'Welcome home,' he said.